The Great Village Bun Fight

Debbie McGowan

Part of
SEASONS OF LOVE
Anthology

Beaten Track
www.beatentrackpublishing.com

ISBN: 978 1 78645 255 9

Church of England Prayer for Same-Sex Marriage taken from http://
www.stmaryandstnicolas.org.uk/prayerssame.html

The Bible Societies (1976) *Good News Bible: Today's English Edition*,
1 Corinthians, 13: verses 1–13, pp. 216–7.

Beaten Track Publishing,
Burscough, Lancashire.
www.beatentrackpublishing.com

Acknowledgements

Many thanks to Reverend John Bennett, Vicar of Spalding, St Mary and St Nicolas, for permitting me to include his suggested prayers and blessing for same-sex couples, and for re-instilling some of my lost faith in Church of England clergy.

As always, thank you to the amazing Beaten Track team— special thanks to Jor for a) proofreading every story I throw your way, often at very short notice, and b) making requests I can successfully and gladly fulfil.

Contents

Begat Henry, Recurring

I N 1874, UPON the birth of his son—and to the chagrin of his father and grandfather, both stonemasons—Henry Jones the Third established *Henry Jones and Son, Baker,* in his home village of Banton, population: 123, all of whom, prior to Henry's entrepreneurial escapades, baked their own bread.

John Porter, Butcher, came soon after, followed by *Albert Thorndike, Tailor and Haberdasher, Edith Forsythe, Grocer,* and countless others who would not stand the rigours and trials of time but nonetheless played their part in putting Banton High Street on the map.

So it came to pass that Henry Jones the Fourth, having inherited both his father's name and business acumen, commenced his apprenticeship in 1889. By 1895, his creations—not least the infamous Banton Bun made to the Joneses' secret family recipe—took pride of place on the bakery shelves. In 1899, he married Josephine the farmer's daughter; a year later, they welcomed Henry the Fifth into the world, who (later) begat Henry, who (much later) begat Henry, who... Well, you get the idea, I'm sure.

Now, successful and influential as the Henry Joneses were, they saw their fair share of strife. Young Henry the Fifth was still wet behind the ears when his father died on a WWI battlefield and, in a cruel repeat of history, failed himself to return from WWII, leaving the bakery in the safe but bellicose hands of newlywed Henry the Sixth, who worked until he dropped dead, right there in front of his own ovens, at the age of fifty.

To the good fortune of all concerned—a staff of no less than a baker's dozen—Henry the Seventh proved a much more placid boss than his father. That is, until it came to his retirement.

As one would expect, Henry begat Henry, but he begat Jennifer and Susan first, and Jennifer and Susan were children of the sixties. Generation X. Riding the second wave

and

Henry Jones

and *Son*

got right

up

their noses.

Not least because said *son*—Henry the Eighth, lest we have forgotten—lost his head. Couldn't happen to a nicer person, you might think, but no. We're talking figuratively, as opposed to some kind of four-centuries-later karmic biting him on the bum just for happening to be the poor begatted bugger who landed that particular incarnation of the family name.

Henry Jones the Eighth. What an idiot, although whether he's more so than his father is the subject of ongoing debate…

***

"Naughty, naughty…"

"Very naughty."

A horn blared, long and loud.

"Shit, them strobes, mate."

"Very naughty... Yeah, don't think we're at the rave no more, Jonesy."

"What's them lights, then—oh, fuck!"

Tripping on the kerb, still tripping in general, they rough-and-tumbled to safety, laughing and crying and serious and crying and laughing and up on their feet, and off they went again.

"Got any matches on you, Mick?"

"Er, yeah." Pat, pat, pockets, chest, pockets. "Somewhere." Matches found. "Here."

"Ta."

"What for?"

"Wanker what just nearly run us over." Parked outside the kebab shop. "Gonna have him." Across the road, to the wanker's car. "His own fault..." Window down. "Should look where he's fucking going."

"Jonesy, what the hell, man?"

Discarded newspaper on the passenger seat. *Strike.*

"Jonesy, don't—"

Whoosh!

"There. That'll teach him."

"What the fuck have you—"

"Run! Fucking run!"

***

Yes, they ran, not very far and not very fast, because... dragons. Big red dragons chasing eighteen-year-old ravers up Banton High Street. Of course, they weren't really dragons, but that's what Henry 'Jonesy' Jones the Eighth will tell you to this day. *We didn't know it was a fucking fire engine, did we? Aceeeeed! Ha-ha. Naughty, that. Good night, though.*

Arson, a five-year-prison sentence…oh, and the conception of Henry the Ninth. A good night, indeed.

To be fair to Henry's father (fairer than he deserves), those darker-crust days brought the comedians out in force—*Is your lad out, then? No? Oh, so it was* you *who burnt the bread*—and the jokes continued right up to his retirement, making a misery of the last ten years of his working life. There was nothing else for it.

"Let us take over, Dad," Jennifer beseeched.

"Then it won't be Henry Jones *and Son*, will it?"

"So change the name," Susan told him. Again.

"No. Can't be doing that. Your great-great—"

"Here we go."

"Dad, we know."

"—great-grandfather would turn in his grave if…"

To cut to the chase: upon his retirement—and to the chagrin of his daughters—Henry Jones the Seventh shut the doors on *Henry Jones and Son, Baker,* leaving the burgeoning village of Banton, population: 900, for the first time in 131 years, without their daily bread.

Firestarter

13 Years Later...
Guy Fawkes Night

L IKE EVERY GUY Fawkes Night since time immemorial, the village green was crammed full of revellers as Bantonions young and old, and all those in between, gathered for fun, fireworks and far too much food. There were fairground games and kiddies' rides, ice cream kiosks and catering vans, all vying for custom with their joyous racket of music, bells, shouts and squeals. The air was crisp, the breeze brisk and sweet with toffee apples, candy floss, roasted chestnuts, potatoes, burgers, hot dogs... The tantalising aroma of caramelised onions set Henry's stomach off in a loud, hungry growl.

Daniel glanced sideways at him and grinned. "Do you want to get something to eat?"

Henry shook his head. "You could get cavities just from breathing tonight."

"Not if you breathe through your nose," Daniel pointed out, to which Henry gave a sad, snotty sniff. "Sorry. I keep forgetting you're sick. Look, we can go home if you want."

Henry rolled his eyes. "Don't be daft. I've only got a cold, and anyway, it's better out than in."

Daniel's grin returned, full force. "I bet you say that to all the boys."

"You'll never know..." Henry tormented in a spooky vibrato that became a shrill "Ouch!" when Daniel squeezed his fingers. A woman walking past frowned at the noise, not looking their way, the frown quickly morphing into a smile when she saw who had made it.

"Evening, you two," she greeted.

"Hi, Ness," both answered, and Henry asked, "How you doing, cuz?"

"Great!" she said through a gritted-teeth smile, the reason for which soon after became apparent.

"Mummy, *please* can I have a toffee appley?"

"I want candy foss!"

Nessa's two kids tugged at her sleeves—one on each.

"We've only just had tea. Let's wait a bit, shall we?"

"But—"

"No."

"I want one *now!*"

"I said no, Kira."

Nessa's five-year-old went into an immediate sulk but didn't argue. Nessa sighed. "Kids," she said.

"Glad I never was one," Henry quipped.

"Yeah. Tell me about it."

Daniel coughed, failing to cover his laughter, but there was no need. Henry's mum was brilliant, but she'd had a hard time looking after him when she was on her own and so young herself, and he'd always tried to be good, not give her any trouble. More than that, he wanted to prove he wasn't like his dad. He wasn't a criminal. He was a responsible graduate with a decent job and a long-term boyfriend. Next year, they would have saved enough for a deposit on a house, and they had big plans. It was why they'd come to Guy

Fawkes Night, or partly why. The other part was that Daniel loved fireworks.

"Ness, Ness! I haven't told you, have I?" She'd started to move away from him but stopped and turned back.

"Told me what?"

Henry's cheeks tingled with the onset of a blush. "Danny and I are…um…we're getting married."

"You're…" Nessa's mouth fell open. "Oh wow! That's awesome!" She threw her arms around them both, squashing them together until they could hardly breathe. Nessa was a big lass and strong. Really, *really* strong.

"Lemme go!" Henry squeaked while Daniel merely looked afraid for his life.

With one final, rib-cracking squeeze, Nessa released them. "I'm so happy for you! Congratulations!"

Henry beamed. "Thanks, Ness."

"If you need me to help with anything…"

"I'm sure there'll be loads of things, but it's sixteen months away yet, and we're still figuring out the logistics, like where to have the ceremony and reception, and…the cake."

***

Freeze-frame.

OK…remember all that *Henry begat Henry begat Henry* that ended when Henry the Eighth set fire to a car outside the kebab shop and was thereby disinherited? Right, well, the good people of Banton still needed their daily bread, and let's just say Henry the Third wasn't the only entrepreneur to ever grace that fine village.

Enter Margaret Sharpe (nee Thatcher, believe it or not), the great-great-granddaughter of Edith Forsythe, our olden-days greengrocer. And she is a sharp one, our Margaret, rightly sharing the name *and* heritage of Britain's first female prime minister.

Just weeks after Henry Jones the Seventh turned his 'Closed' sign for the final time, Margaret Sharpe had *The Village Bakery & Grocery* up and running faster than you can say 'I'll have a small batch and a couple of floury baps'.

More on that later…

***

"Ah," Nessa said knowingly. All their family weddings so far, their grandad had made the cakes, but at seventy-seven, he was a bit forgetful and not in the best health, and Henry and Daniel didn't want to be a bother to him.

"Yeah, so," Henry continued, "we're going to ask Margaret."

"Uh-huh?"

Henry nodded. And waited. When Nessa said nothing further, he prompted, "Bad idea?"

"No. Well…she can only say no."

"That's what worries me."

All three glanced over to the food vans, parked in a line, at the end of which was a gazebo adorned with a façade transforming it into a miniature Houses of Parliament—guaranteed by history to be the one thing left standing at the end of the night should the carnival atmosphere get out of hand.

"We could go and see her now, while it's quiet," Daniel suggested.

"Good idea," Henry agreed—out loud. He was still hoping for a medical miracle to restore his grandad's youthful vigour, but he said *au revoir* to his cousin and let Daniel lead him by the hand over to Lady Margaret's grand stall.

Unnoticed by the proprietor, they watched her ice a smiley face and scarf onto a gingerbread man, and then another, and another... They could be there a while.

"Those look delicious," Daniel gushed to alert her to their presence. She startled and lynched a gingerbread man by his sugar scarf.

"Good heavens! What a fright you gave me, boys!" Casting her icing bag aside, she wiped her hands on a tea towel, nose crinkled in a grimace as she tugged the terry fabric to unstick it from her palm. "What would you like? I've some lovely moist parkin—" she pointed to a tray containing a slab of very dark brown cake "—as good as your grandfather's, I dare say..." In lieu of raising an eyebrow, she part-closed one eye, head wobbling with her boast. "Or perhaps some coconut ice? How about this delicious creamy vanilla fudge made with fresh dairy cream. Or—"

"A gingerbread man for me, please." Daniel cut off her inventory recital.

"I also have gingerbread ladies," Margaret singsonged. To prove it, she delicately lifted a beskirted ginger person from the tray and held it aloft, wafting her free hand in illustration of her craft.

"Either works for me," Daniel replied so solemnly Henry turned away to battle the guffaw set to explode from him with at least the velocity of the rockets set to imminently decorate the skies.

"A lady for you, Henry dear?" Margaret prompted. She wasn't selling confectionery; she was selling brides. That was when he knew for sure theirs was a lost cause, but they'd come this far.

"Too much biscuit," he muttered out of the side of his mouth, followed by a louder, firmer, "That would be lovely, thanks, Mrs. Sharpe." He even managed a controlled smile to go with it. "Actually…" He focused on the discarded icing bag as he spoke. "We came to ask you…" *Big breath.* "Something."

"Did you now?" She handed Daniel his biscuit but kept Henry's hostage.

"Yes, um… We wondered if… Well, see, we're getting married, and—"

***

So, here's the thing. That comparison of our Margaret to the formidable Mrs. Thatcher? It wasn't accidental. Margaret is…for the sake of politeness, let's call her 'traditional'. Family values, individual liberty, the free market—Conservative with a capital C—and yes, she *was* responsible for organising the Banton street party to celebrate Mrs. T's election win in 1979, amongst other things, but that was her shining moment. She even took home the Union Jack bunting and insisted Mr. Sharpe hang it around the garden. These days, it's a tad faded and frayed around the pointy ends, but there it will stay until they commit Margaret's mortal remains to the earth, because you can bet your sweet bippy she'll be taking it with her.

While most Bantonions have moved with the times, sadly our Margaret isn't one of them. This lady is most certainly not for turning. Turnovers? You might be in with a chance.

You can probably figure out where this is going…

***

"—we wondered if you'd make our wedding cake."
Silence.

Above the houses at the back of the green, a rocket launched optimistically, sprayed the sky with a spatter of green, and *pff*'d out of existence.

Slowly, and with great dread, Henry shifted his eyes left and up, up, up, meeting the judgemental glare first of the gingerbread woman, which was bad enough, and then of Margaret, except her expression was less judgement than disappointment.

In the near distance, a Catherine Wheel whizz-whizz-whizzed in a frenzy. Sparklers popped and crackled, and Postman Pat completed another revolution of the kids' merry-go-round.

At last, Margaret broke her silence with a heavy sigh. "Oh dear." She handed over Henry's gingerbread woman and waved away Daniel's offer of payment. "How old are you now, boys? Twenty-two?"

"Yes," Daniel confirmed. He was getting annoyed, Henry could tell from the weary, talking-to-an-idiot tone he'd developed since they'd returned from university to their home village only to hear the same thing over and over again—

Haven't you put that nonsense behind you?

It's about time you both grew up.

You just need to meet the right girls, settle down...

—no matter that they'd been together since they were sixteen.

"No," Margaret said. "I'm sorry. The day God allows you to marry in His church—"

"Reverend Osbourne has given us his blessing," Daniel argued.

Margaret laughed, all high-pitched and ridiculous. "He is not *God*."

"He's a man of God, though, and if the Church would let him, he'd marry us."

"Hmm." She tilted her head back so she was looking down her nose at them.

"Come on." Henry grabbed Daniel by the arm and pulled him away, too angry to stay and fight. There was no point, and he didn't want her rotten cake anyway.

Of course, she still had to say her piece, loudly calling after them, "I love you boys dearly, but I cannot condone your choices."

Henry took a vicious bite and decapitated his gingerbread woman.

"I'll say a prayer for you on Sunday," Margaret offered.

"Yeah, don't," Daniel muttered and thrust his biscuit at Nessa, who intercepted them halfway across the green.

"I was coming to rescue you," she said.

Henry shook his head. He didn't want to dissect their conversation with Margaret, such as it could be called that.

In silence, the three of them walked over to the area cordoned off with fluorescent orange rope, beyond which half a dozen men were lining up the first of the fireworks. "What have you done with the kids?" Henry asked.

"On the teacups." She thumbed behind her. "With Grandad."

"Oh! He's here?"

"Obviously."

"Isn't it a bit chilly for him to be out? And he's on a fairground ride? He could fall off or anything!"

Nessa sighed in exasperation. "It's a kids' ride, Henry, and he's really not that frail. You know—"

"Don't, Ness."

"Don't what?"

"Don't say it."

She took a bite of gingerbread and crunched noisily, which was as good as saying it. *Ask Grandad to make your cake.* It was bad enough that *that woman* had stolen his grandad's business…well, she hadn't. If Henry's dad hadn't been such a let-down, or if his grandad had been less stubborn… because, in a way, he was no better than Margaret when it came to 'respecting tradition'. The world wouldn't have ended if *Henry Jones and Son* had become *Henry Jones and Daughter* or just *Henry Jones, Baker*…

"Looks like we're ready for lift-off," Daniel said.

"He's on his way over," Nessa said.

"Can I have a toffee appley now, Mummy?" Kira said.

Henry only vaguely heard them. Only vaguely noticed his grandad come to stand next to him. Only vaguely saw the fireworks.

Don't make problems, create solutions. That's what his boss said, pretty much every day. Cheesy, yes, but Henry liked his job. It paid well, and he'd already had one promotion.

"Dan?"

The crowd *ooooohed.*

"Mmm?"

And the crowd *aaaahed.*

"I want to go self-employed."

"Doing?"

"*Henry Jones, Baker, est. 1874.*"

A rocket spluttered and launched, and Henry and Daniel watched it shoot high into the sky.

"She's really upset you, hasn't she?"

"Yep, and maybe it's a stupid idea. I mean, I don't know anything about baking."

Above them, the rocket loudly exploded in a shower of red sparks.

"But you know a man who does," Daniel said, peering past Henry and then right at him as he sought out his hand and gave it an encouraging squeeze. "Go for it."

Henry nodded, grateful for Daniel's support. Drawing a long, shaky breath, he pivoted to face the man on his other side. "Grandad?"

"Aye, lad?"

"Are you busy?"

A deep, bushy-browed frown was his answer.

Henry chuckled, suddenly full of nerves, and crossed his fingers. "I've got a favour to ask. Well, two, actually…"

Tricycle, Icycle

The Following Winter...
Christmas Eve

DO WHAT YOU *do best.*

So said Henry's grandad a year ago to the day as he handed Henry a small, red-foil-wrapped box that gave a metallic rattle when he shook it. Inside: a large bunch of mismatched keys held together by a ring the size of a bangle.

The keys to the bakery.

Henry's bakery.

No going back. Definitely not after Margaret changed the sign on her shop so it read:

THE Village Bakery & Grocery
Home of the Banton Bun

Not THE Banton Bun, mind you—Margaret doesn't have the Joneses' secret family recipe—but a reasonable approximation.

As for Henry doing what he does best... Henry Jones the Ninth is no baker, that's for sure. He wouldn't even know how to assemble a Banton Bun, let alone bake one. But he *does* know his way around computers, accounts, managing staff and stock inventory. And he rides a mean tricycle.

You might wonder how that could be a good thing. Read on, and all will be revealed.

***

"Have you seen?"

Henry slapped his hand down on the paperwork to anchor it against the icy gust that rushed into the bakery—along with a pink, panting Nessa—and set the Christmas tree bead strings into a wave of tsunami proportions. Nessa whipped her umbrella shut, javelined it into the stand and frivolously kicked the door with her heel. The force wasn't quite enough to shut it—luckily.

Mrs. Broughton was a step behind her and whinnied, pulled up short by the obstruction between her and her weekly egg—*free range, of course*—custard tart. Nessa didn't appear to notice and scurried around the end of the counter, unfastening and pulling off her coat on her way past Henry.

"Have I seen wh—"

"*Not now!*" she hissed, disappearing out back then reappearing a second later, still pink and panting, with her *Henry Jones, Baker, est. 1874* apron dangling from her neck, hands labouring at her back and a big, false smile for their customer. "Good morning, Mrs. B. How are you today?" She side-eyed a further warning for Henry to keep his mouth shut until they were on their own.

"Oh, you know how it is." Mrs. Broughton wearily rubbed her left wrist and then her right with gnarled old fingers sporting freshly manicured, glittery red nails. Evidently, the bakery wasn't her first stop of the morning.

"Your arthritis giving you trouble, is it?" Nessa simpered. No time to waste on small talk when she had gossip to impart, she tugged a brown paper—*recycled, it goes without saying*—bag free of the hemp string and flicked it open.

"It is, love," Mrs. Broughton lamented. "Still, it's to be expected with the damp and the cold." She glowered in disapproval.

Henry peered out the front window at the drizzly gloom. "Snow's on its way," he mused aloud.

"Don't say that!" Mrs. Broughton chastised, aghast.

"According to the—ouch!" Nessa stamped on his toes. "BBC," he finished obstinately.

"Aye, well, what do they know about the weather?"

"The Met Office too—ow!" Henry inhaled sharply at the stamp on his other foot and shut up for good this time. Not his snowflakes, not his blizzard.

Nessa raised the serving tongs and crocodile-snapped the air. "One or two-tart day today, Mrs. B.?"

"Two, please. I have to entertain the Reverend Osbourne this afternoon." She patted her hair and honked out a heavy sigh. "I could do without the rigmarole on Christmas Eve, I must confess."

Nessa muted a snort and got to transferring two egg custards from glass cabinet to bag. Henry cleared his throat and faked concentrating on his paperwork. Better Mrs. Broughton think them rude than realise they were laughing, although not at her, or not *just* at her. Most of the older village folk thought their young vicar, with his long hair and love of rock music, was a lout. If only they took the time to get to know him, they'd realise what a lovely guy he was. Well, Henry thought so. Nessa just wanted to get into his pants.

Mrs. Broughton had a soft spot for him too, regardless of her 'could do without the rigmarole' of the manicure and, Henry observed, new hairdo. She was the long-standing, completely unbudgeable and somewhat dictatorial leader of the Parish Council, of which Margaret Sharpe had been secretary until a few months ago. Suffice to say, she now knew why Mrs. Broughton—and other members—had

stopped buying cakes from THE Village Bakery, and it had
nothing to do with calorie-counting or diabetes.

Nessa twisted the corners of the paper bag and set it on
the counter. "Anything else, Mrs. B.?"

"No, that's it, love. How much do I owe you?" She clicked
open her purse and tinkled the loose change inside.

"Two pounds twenty, please."

"Have they gone up again?" They hadn't, as well Mrs.
Broughton knew, but she had to say it. Every week. "Eeeeee,
I don't know how they expect us to live on a pittance of a
pension, cost of living being what it is and all. Here, love. I
can't get hold of the little so-and-sos with these nails."

Without warning, she upended her purse. Nessa swooped
in with a well-aimed palm and caught most of the coins
before they hit the glass top of the cake cabinet. A two-
pence piece bounced off and rolled across the floor, coming
to a stop next to Henry's bruised toes. He retrieved it and
rose to return it to their customer.

"Stick it in the Sally Army tin, love," Mrs. Broughton
ordained, clicking her purse shut and zipping her coat right
up under her chin, creating a dimple in her crinkles, but
at least she'd be warm. She gathered her wares. "I'll be off,
then. A Merry Christmas to you."

"And to you," Henry called.

"Yeah, and you, Mrs. B." Nessa wide-eye-watched her
all the way to the door, which she fought with a fierce
determination when the wind flung it open and refused to
relinquish its hold. Nessa dashed over to help and, between
them, they managed to put wood back in t'hole before Mrs.
Broughton set off at a fair old speed.

Nessa gave a conspiratorial glance up and down the high
street before she returned to the counter. "Soooo…" she
said, eyebrows arched to embellish the suspense.

Henry nonchalantly dropped the tuppence into the Shelter—not Salvation Army—collection tin and straightened the paper bags. "So?"

"You haven't seen it?"

"Depends."

"On?"

"What you're talking about."

"The notice."

He shrugged. "Outside the camping shop?"

Now is the winter
Of our discount tents

Henry thought it was hilarious.

"Not *that* one," Nessa said. "On the noticeboard?"

"Good place for it," Henry quipped. Nessa folded her arms and glared. Henry grinned. "No, I haven't seen *the notice*. Not that I know of."

"Well!" Nessa unfolded her arms again and rubbed her hands in glee, back on track with the juicy gossip. She went over to the coffee jug. "Is this fresh?" she asked, already pouring a cup.

"Made just before you got here," Henry confirmed.

She turned to face him, sipped coffee, smacked her lips. Either she was building up to something big or was worried about his reaction. Still he refused to prompt her further and instead reached for his paperwork, his fingers grazing the top sheet as she finally relented.

"Hold that," she said and thrust her cup at him so she could get her phone from her pocket. "I took a photo of it on my way out."

"Out of where?"

"The village hall."

"Is playschool on today?"

"If it's not, Marky'll be sitting on his lonesome for the morning." She unlocked the screen, and they did a quick, awkward swap of items.

She'd taken one of those pictures that refused to stay upright, and Henry had to hold the phone at a jaunty angle, with his head tipped to the side, to read the notice. He didn't even make it past the headline before his stomach did a somersault. "No way." He shoved Nessa's phone back at her. "No. Way!"

"We'll easily win," she goaded.

"We won't, because we're not entering."

"Why not?"

"Are you kidding me?"

"Friendly competition…"

"Friendly? Remember the Easter Bonnets? I told you it was too soon."

"We were more than ready to take her on."

"I don't *want* to take her on!" Henry snapped.

"Really?" Nessa questioned. "Because that's not how it looks. OK, I know we're *artisan* and *catering for a different demographic*—" he couldn't believe she'd air-quoted at him—twice! "—but *you* re-opened the bakery."

"Yep, and have you noticed she's gone all 'free range, organic' la-de-dah? She doesn't give a hoot about ethical sourcing or hens' well-being. She's just an out-and-out copycat." Henry picked up his pile of papers, tapped them to straighten them, put them down again and propped his hand on his hip.

Beside him, Nessa took a breath and paused, as if she were considering saying more, but merely huffed a, "Fine, whatever," and stormed out the back.

That was where she stayed for the next three hours, only emerging to help in the busy periods. Henry was surprised so many villagers had braved the increasingly bleak weather to pick up a Christmas Eve treat—weather which, sooner rather than later, he was going to have to brave himself. He still needed to get out with the deliveries.

By twelve-thirty, when he could stand the dramatic thumps and bangs no more, he prepared a peace offering of leek and potato—*vegan, locally sourced*—soup plus a couple of sourdough—*baked in-house*—rolls and tentatively approached the kitchen, loitering in the doorway to watch his cousin's purposeful march back and forth with sundry items, all destined for the delivery trailer. She slotted three French batons into a corner and made brief eye contact, her scowl still firmly in place.

"I've brought lunch," he said, holding it up as evidence.

"Thanks." She marched off to the storeroom—*bang, clatter, grunt*—and returned with four jars of cranberry jelly. Into the trailer they went.

"Will I be in your way if—"

"No."

He was in the way simply by being there. To avoid upsetting her further, he dodged around the centre island to the microwave and stayed with it while the soup warmed, pretending to look around the room when he was watching Nessa, yet over those few moments, his focus shifted and he started thinking about the kitchen instead. He'd felt more welcome there as a mischievous kid getting in his grandad's way than he did now, and not just because of Nessa's mood, which was still icier than the chilly December afternoon.

He missed the baking. It wasn't like it didn't happen, but it didn't happen while he was on the premises. By eight a.m., when Henry arrived, the baker was done, leaving only dozens of loaves lined up on the racks and the residual heat of the ovens. At this time of year, he appreciated the warmth, especially first thing; come spring and summer, it was…well, like an oven.

For all that Henry's name was above the door, it wasn't his bakery, and not because—secretly—he and Nessa were equal partners. Henry could manage staff, do the accounts, cash up, clean up, take care of the deliveries, but when it came to the real work—baking bread and serving customers—he was clueless. It hadn't troubled him until today.

Until Nessa showed him that notice.

"I'm done," she mumbled and flopped sulkily onto a stool. "What soup is it?"

"Leek and potato." The microwave pinged and he removed the bowl, shoving it in front of her. "Here." He edged past and out of the kitchen.

"Are you not having any?" she called.

"Nope." Yanking his coat from the hook, he struggled into it on his way back. "Not hungry. I'm gonna get the deliveries out before it gets any colder." *Hat on, gloves…*

"Where's your helmet?"

…*delivery chits…* "Can't wear it with a hat."

"Henry—" The rumble of the rising bay door cut off her warning.

Henry lugged the trailer out into the yard, calling, "See you later," through the slowly diminishing gap as the door rolled shut.

***

All right, let's take stock here. We've got a loaded trailer, a Henry agitated to the point of recklessness, icy roads and a tricycle. That, folks, is what we call an accident waiting to happen. And the thing is, Henry's not really angry with

Nessa. If she hadn't told him about the contest, someone else would've done. Indeed, by the time he's done with this fateful Christmas Eve (that's fateful, *not* fatal—one wedding and no funerals, I promise), almost everyone in Banton will have asked him if *Henry Jones, Baker, est. 1874* is doing it.

'Doing what?' you may ask. Well.

The clue's in the title, innit?

OK. Christmas Eve tricycling on ice. Are you sitting comfortably? Good, because Henry most definitely is not.

***

For the first hour or so—in spite of a slightly deflated back-left tyre and arm-ache from compensating for the subsequent veer gutterwards—Henry made good progress, fuelled by the systematic renewal of his annoyance each time he heard 'Have you seen the poster? Are you going to enter?' On the plus side, he got a pleasant surprise around the halfway point when he discovered the next address on the list was his own. Daniel had been watching through the front window and came out to help.

"Don't say it," Henry warned.

Daniel took the bags from him. "I wasn't going to say anything."

"We're not entering."

"We are talking about the Cake-Off, aren't we?"

Henry grunted and took off his hat to scratch his hot head. Tricycling with a fully loaded trailer was hard work. "You know whose idea that is, don't you?"

"It wasn't Margaret's," Daniel said.

"Pshure."

"Honestly. It's the talk of the village."

"Yeah, I noticed," Henry grumbled. "I can't wait to get finished today." He eyed the remaining six deliveries in his trailer. "So, who came up with that brilliance?"

"The vicar."

Henry was horrified. "You'd think he'd be encouraging his parishioners to get along, not forcing us to compete with each other."

"Did you actually read the poster, Hen?"

"Yes. Well…no. It was on Ness's phone—too small—but whatever. I saw enough. I'm not going up against Margaret Sharpe." With more force than was necessary, Henry pulled his hat on, scowling under the pressure both of the woollen band half-covering his eyes and Daniel's continued surveillance. "What?" he snapped and shoved the hat up his forehead.

"You wouldn't be going up *against* Margaret."

"That's exactly what I just said! No way are we entering that competition. Absolutely n— Wait. What did you say?"

"You're not going up against Margaret."

"Why not?"

"Because, my sweet, lovely, totally unflustered and entirely reasonable darling, it's an inter-village contest. Judging is at the County Fair on May Day."

"The County… An inter…" Henry's indignation diminished to soundless lip-flapping.

***

If he wasn't horrified before, he certainly is now. What's worse than competing against THE Village Bakery? Competing *with* them. Of course, he could just say no, but that wouldn't be much of a story, would it?

***

"No." Henry hurried into his gloves, and out of them again to get the requisite fingers in the requisite…fingers.

"Hen…" Daniel beseeched.

"Got to finish these deliveries." He planted a quick kiss on Daniel's chilled lips—"Home by five, love you"—straddled the trike and set off at a pace for his next drop.

Black ice.

Up ahead.

He didn't see it in time to avoid it, naturally. That's why it's called *black* ice. And if there's a positive to come out of this, the trike's brakes were as responsive as one could possibly hope for. Pity they didn't come with ABS.

Slam on, jackknifed trailer, headfirst over the handlebars…

Henry crumpled to the ground amid a grisly mess of French batons and cranberry jelly.

"Like severed limbs all over the road, it were," an eyewitness told the *Banton Gazette*.

First on scene, Mrs. Margaret Sharpe [proprietor of THE Village Bakery] whose home is adjacent to the site of the accident, tended to the injured Mr. Jones and ~~smothered~~ wrapped him in blankets to keep him warm while awaiting the ambulance.

Mr. Jones was later discharged by the hospital, into his fiancé's care, with cuts and bruises and a slight concussion. He [begrudgingly] expresses his gratitude to Mrs. Sharpe for ensuring he didn't get hypothermia and lived to celebrate another Christmas.

Flipping Out

Early Spring...
Shrove Tuesday

Y OU'RE GETTING MARRIED *in four hours... Ding dong, the bells are gonna chime...*" Aunty Jen sang and sashayed into the bakery kitchen with another empty tray.

Henry covered his ears and grimaced. Jen nudged him with her hip, knocking his pencil out of his hand and onto the floor. Still humming her ditty, she picked up the pencil and returned it to him before repeating the same two tuneless lines as she filled the sink with scalding-hot water.

"Four more hours and you'll never have to listen to her dying-cat routine again," Nessa muttered as she passed Henry on her way to the pantry. "And we're nearly out of crêpes." She disappeared from view, reappearing less than thirty seconds later, clutching a cellophane-wrapped tray. "This is the last dozen."

"It's not even lunchtime," Henry pointed out, already mentally running through the options. Yes, he and Daniel were getting married today—the anniversary of the day they came out, together, to their families, which, *coincidentally*, had fallen on Shrove Tuesday and did *not*, in any way, symbolise their enduring mutual love of pancakes—but not for another four, pancake-less hours. "What are we going to do?"

"We'll just have to send people to Margaret's," Nessa suggested, quickly retreating to the shop.

Henry didn't want to do that. He didn't suppose Nessa did either, but what choice did they have? Henry's last attempt at pancakes was basically scrambled eggs, Nessa didn't have time in between serving customers, and there was no point even asking Aunty Jen. She'd only come to collect serving dishes—she'd sworn she'd never set foot in the bakery again—but instead was helping out and intermittently torturing Henry through the medium of song.

She turned towards him, drying the tray. "Are you going home soon?"

"How can I? We sold out of Scotch pancakes by ten o'clock this morning. Now we're nearly out of crêpes. It's a disaster! The pancake apocalypse!"

Aunty Jen laughed. "Well, at least you'll know for next year."

"If we're still in business. *She's* going to steal all our customers, and win the Cake-Off, and probably get an OBE for her contribution to the industry. *And* I let her have exclusive selling rights on the Banton Bun. It's so unfair."

"Oh, Henry." Aunty Jen's laughter had gone full-belly. "I think you might be making a bit of a mountain out of a molehill, but you know, it's not too late to join forces."

"With that...that *cutthroat*? After what she did last Easter? Never!"

***

The previous year...

Easter Saturday: a grand day for an opening! Spring had sprung spectacularly. The sun shone, birds sang, and Henry and Nessa had everything they needed for their Easter Bonnet competition. Or *not really* a competition. There were prizes for *all* the children, a free taster buffet with wine for the adults...

...and the proprietor of THE Village Bakery was livid. LIVID, I tells ya. Oh, she'd heard the gossip; she only had to step out of her premises to see the preparations taking place a few yards along the high street. But she'd refused to believe it, even when Henry told her to her face—

"I'm re-opening my grandad's business. Artisan bread and pastries, organic, free-range ingredients sourced from local producers. Rest assured, Mrs. Sharpe, I have no intention of competing with you."

—until the day came when she could deny it no longer.

On Easter Saturday, to Margaret Sharpe's tremendous chagrin, Henry Jones the Ninth opened the doors on *Henry Jones, Baker, est. 1874*, providing the commuter-belt village of Banton, population: 1,500, for the first time ever, with a choice of where to buy their daily bread.

Villagers flocked from far and wide (OK, not very far and not very wide, it's not *that* big a village) to taste Henry the Hipster's fantastic new baked goods while a mardy-faced Margaret watched on from the doorway of her deserted shop. There was nothing else for it.

She bustled back inside and got straight on the phone to Mr. Sharpe, putting him immediately to work on the new signage, but the icing on the cake—a poor pun in the circumstances, I appreciate—was her answer to Henry and Nessa's Easter Bonnet and Buffet.

Complimentary chocolate egg
with every Easter Saturday purchase
if accompanied by child

"It's a free market," Margaret later defended to Henry's Aunty Jen (who, incidentally, has a Master's degree in economics and is also a bit nifty with a frying pan and a gallon of pancake batter—relevant but problematic, as we shall see).

"Free market, my arse," said Jen, eloquently, like the scholar she is.

"Simple supply and demand, *Ms. Jones*. The invisible hand ensures resources are allocated efficiently. Banton is too small to sustain two bakeries—"

"Just as well, *Mrs. Sharpe*, because my visible hands are going to wring your visible bloody neck."

***

"What d'you think you're doing?"

The bakery back door swung wide open. Henry and Aunty Jen stopped talking and stared at their visitor like headlight-illuminated wildlife.

Tick, tock, tick, tock,
Just a lil ol' clock,
I'm here all the time,
But these seconds are mine.
Tick, tock, TICK, TOCK!

"I, um…" Henry fidgeted and almost toppled off his stool. "Hello, Grandad."

"Never mind that. Why are you here?"

"Why wouldn't I be?"

Grandad raised his arm with slow deliberation, squinted at his watch and nodded. "Tuesday. Thought so."

Henry chuckled nervously. His grandad was a sarcastic sod when the mood took.

"Get yourself off home, lad. Even I took us wedding day off."

Aunty Jen's mouth fell open. "You lying swine!"

"What do *you* know? You weren't there."

"Don't believe a word of it," Jen said to Henry. "He told your gran she could set any date she liked as long as it was a Wednesday."

Grandad shoved his hands in his trouser pockets and gave a little shrug. "Aye. Half-day closing. No point wasting it."

"See?" Henry grinned smugly.

"Oh, I see, all right," Jen said. "Two stubborn buggers called Henry."

Nessa reappeared with the tray she'd taken through not two minutes ago, now empty. "Comes with the name, I reckon."

"Listen," Henry interjected as firmly as he dared. "I can't go anywhere till we've figured out what to do about the crêpes."

"Crêpes?"

"Pancakes, Grandad."

"I'm well aware, lad. What about 'em?"

"We've run out," Nessa said.

"So make some more."

"Ah. Well." Henry cleared his throat. "I don't know how."

"What kind of baker doesn't know how to make a pancake?" Before Henry could answer—and 'you don't bake pancakes, you fry them' would have done him no favours anyway—Grandad nodded at Aunty Jen. "She knows how."

"Who's she? The cat's mother?" Aunty Jen muttered and shook her head. "Sorry, Hen, I'm not making them—" she glowered at her dad "—on *principle*."

Grandad grunted. "For goodness' sake. That again? It's not as if he's asking you to run the place."

"He wouldn't bloody dare, would he? Not with you sticking your oar in every five minutes."

"Oy! Watch your tone with me, young lady…"

Henry shrank as small as could be on his stool, but it was nowhere near small enough when not there at all would have been his ideal.

"Watch my tone?!" Jen yelled back, advancing on her father. "You're damn lucky I still talk to you at all. Our Susan had the right idea."

Nessa edged along the wall like a burglar and jerked her head to get Henry's attention, rolling her eyes meaningfully towards the back door. He nodded his understanding and made a run for it.

"This has been brewing for years," she said, once they were safely out in the courtyard where the argument was just as loud but with enough distance that neither could be dragged into it.

Henry sighed. "I know. But couldn't they have left it till *after* the wedding?"

"Maybe it'll clear the air a bit," Nessa placated, which was optimistic at best. And maybe it would—between Grandad and Aunty Jen, but not with Aunty Susan, who hadn't spoken to her dad in thirteen years. Then, of course, there was Henry's dad…

***

By now, it will come as no surprise when I tell you that Banton has always prided itself on being a traditional, tranquil little hamlet, a homogeneous, harmonious community of ordinary folk going about their ordinary lives. Henry Jones the Eighth hasn't been welcomed there since the Night of Fire and Dragons that brought shame upon his once well-respected family and resulted in the biggest upheaval in village history.

But take a fingernail to that veneer and scratch just a little beneath the surface, and what've we got?

Henry and Daniel—two young men in love whose families, supportive as they are, advised them to set up home in Anywhere But Banton.

Margaret—OK, her politics might be a bit skewed and her beliefs need a damn good shake-up, but let's give some credit where it's due. She's the *only* female proprietor on Banton High Street, fighting tooth and claw to keep her livelihood.

As for Henry's dad? Well, he wasn't the first Bantonion to go off the rails and he most likely won't be the last. Can we really lay the blame for all of this at his feet?

Idiot that he is, he's still had the good sense to keep his distance. So far…

***

"D'you think they've killed each other?" Henry whispered.

"Possible." Nessa cocked her ear. The fighting had stopped some time ago, and all was quiet. She hopped down from the back of the retired trike—still with buckled wheels— and crept towards the building, pausing at the kitchen door to listen. "I'm going in," she said.

"I'll cover you," Henry said.

"No, you won't. You need to go home and get ready."

"But the bakery—"

Nessa spun on the spot and bumped noses with him. She didn't back off, and neither did he. "My mum's right, you're as bad as Grandad."

"That's not very nice."

"It's the truth," Nessa contended.

Henry blinked and turned away, hurt by her words. He loved his grandad, looked up to him, but he wasn't blind to his faults, like his stupid sexism that led him to shut down the family business rather than hand it over to his daughters—the same sexism that had Henry and Nessa lying to the entire family. He was fed up with it—the lies, the constant battles with Margaret, all of it, and today of all days, the stress was too much.

Frustrated, upset, Henry couldn't help it; he started to cry. "I wish we hadn't bothered."

"With the pancakes?"

"Everything," he sniffled angrily.

Nessa appeared in front of him. "Ohh…Hen." Her expression softened, and she lugged him in for a hug. "I'm so sorry. I didn't mean to upset you."

"It's OK, it wasn't you," Henry wheezed within the squeeze. "I should've stood up to him, told him what we'd planned from the beginning. You're right. I am as bad as him."

"*Stubborn* as him," Nessa corrected.

"Not what you said."

"'s what I meant." She hugged him harder, sniffling a little herself. Henry was sure he was turning blue.

"Ness?"

"Yes, Hen?"

"Can't breathe."

She laugh-cried and released him, straightening his shirt front out of habit. He wiped his eyes on his sleeve and attempted a smile. She kissed his cheek. "It's not all bad, Hen. Really. Just an emotional day. When you get back from your honeymoon, we should have a business meeting, work out what we're going to do, yes?"

"Yes," Henry said.

"In the meantime, I can handle this—them—so *please* go and get ready for your wedding."

"Fine. I'll go…just as soon as I know everything's OK here."

"I swear to God…" Nessa hissed but didn't stop him from following her in, though they barely made it through the door before both tumbled to a halt in time to watch their grandad give a sharp flick of the wrist, send a pancake several feet into the air and then effortlessly catch it in the pan.

Returning it to the stove, he acknowledged Henry and Nessa with a nod. "All right, you two?"

"You made all those while we were outside?" Henry asked, indicating the tray next to the stove. It held at least a dozen pancakes.

"Aye, lad."

"Where's Mum?" Nessa asked.

"Out front, manning the counter." Grandad slid the cooked pancake onto the tray and poured more batter into the pan. "Womanning the counter," he corrected. "I heard you, by the way. What you were talking about in the yard."

Henry and Nessa both mouthed an *oh* and dipped their heads.

"It's hard for you young'uns to understand, but I did what I had to—what I thought was right. As you know, my dad took over this place after the war. He was the same age as you, near as damn it—" he glanced at Henry, paused to flip the pancake, and continued "—and he didn't want it. He'd not long married my mother, and they'd planned to emigrate, but his mother and aunt insisted, said they hadn't kept the bakery going during the war just for him to sell up and ship out. So he did as he was told, and made sure the world knew how bloody miserable he was into the bargain."

Another pancake made, more batter into the pan.

"It was the same for me when he died. Hobson's Choice. I was happy enough, though, fulfilling my obligations, but I didn't want to put that same pressure on my son. I let him do his own thing." The pancake flip was less enthusiastic this time, lifting only enough to turn it over. "At eighteen, I was in bed by seven, in here by three in the morning, six days a week." Grandad sighed, deep and wistful. "I should've brought him in, got him working. It'd have kept him on the straight and narrow."

"You don't know that," Henry said. "Not for sure."

"No, I suppose not." Grandad slid the pancake onto the tray with the rest. "Here, lad. Your turn."

"Oh! Um…" Henry looked to Nessa in panic and could've thumped her when she just nodded in encouragement. "But I'm getting married in…eek! Two hours!"

With that, Henry dashed from the bakery, not even stopping to gather his belongings. As the door shut behind him, he heard Nessa say, "Nice one, Grandad. I thought he was never going to leave!"

***

While Henry races home to prepare for his suddenly impending nuptials, let's review, briefly, the Jones' family dynamic, because there are an awful lot of hesitant Henrys in there. Indeed, it would seem that Henry incumbent is the first to have willingly taken the oven gloves—so to speak—since the original *Henry Jones and Son, Baker.*

One might expect, given young Henry's sense of displacement and minor feelings of baking-related inadequacy, he'd have leapt at the opportunity to pick up a few tricks of the trade from his grandad, as opposed to legging it—a snap decision he's regretting already and he's only just turned off the high street.

As for Nessa...well, she's certainly got her head screwed on, hasn't she? I suspect it comes from being the eldest of the four cousins and a single mum to boot. No real drama there—just one of those 'wasn't meant to be' situations—which is as well when the Joneses as a whole could benefit from a few group sessions with their local therapist (great guy, incidentally, though he wouldn't thank me for the recommendation).

Now, up to this point, Nessa's stayed out of family politics. Sure, she takes after her mother, and doesn't shy away from saying it like it is, but she's more peacekeeper than warrior, which is why she agreed to keep quiet about the bakery joint venture...

...until after the wedding.

Yep. In a few hours, it'll all be over bar the shouting, but even waiting that long is getting to be a stretch. Nessa's old enough to remember the fallout between her mum, Aunty Susan and Grandad. Crucially, she's old enough to remember the party her grandparents threw to celebrate Uncle Henry's release from prison...and their disappointment when he showed no signs of remorse or reform. Never mind that both daughters graduated with honours, successfully pursued careers, set up homes and are caring, responsible parents. If there had been any expectations made of them, they would surely have surpassed every last one.

Sadly, the only thing that ever mattered was handing down the bakery from father to son, father to son, even though Henry Jones the Eighth is still an idiot who never accepts responsibility for his actions and makes promises he can't possibly keep, like, for instance, saying he won't cause trouble at his son's wedding when his mere presence will provoke a kick-off of epic proportions.

Poor young Henry. His mind has been in turmoil since he fled the bakery, his steps becoming slower the closer he gets to home. He wants to get married. He really does, but…

***

"I wish we'd eloped." Henry pushed the front door shut with his bottom and sighed so heavily his back crackled like popcorn.

Daniel appeared, fastening his shirt cuffs, at the top of the stairs. "What did you say?"

"Why didn't we elope? Or better still, never move back here in the first place?"

"Ah." Daniel nodded knowingly. "Are you coming up or shall I come down?"

Henry shook his head and pushed away from the door, using the momentum to climb the stairs. He stopped in front of his husband-to-be and attempted a smile. "You look very handsome."

"Thank you. As do you, Mr. Bun the Baker, but we went to the trouble of buying these suits, so…" Daniel gestured grandly towards their bedroom. "This way, sir. I have something for you."

"Danny…" Henry groaned. He wasn't in the mood, but Daniel just laughed and grabbed his hand, pulling him along, straight past the bedroom to the bathroom. "Oh my…" Henry stared at the bath, then at Daniel, then back at the bath—not the scratched-enamel antiquity that had been there when he'd left for work that morning. "Where…? How…?"

"My wedding gift to you."

Henry smirked. "Just for me?"

Daniel tilted his head from side to side. "OK. For us. Later. I'll leave you to it." Delivering a quick kiss to Henry's cheek, he departed.

"I won't be long," Henry called after him, already tugging his shirt over his head and stamping his way out of his trousers, eager to submerge himself in the ocean-blue, decadently scented water. He oohed and hissed—it was a little on the warm side—as he settled against the back rest, experimentally poking at the closest button on the control panel and getting it right first time. The water erupted all around him in tickly bubbles that made him giggle. He heard an answering laugh from Daniel and closed his eyes, smiling as his earlier worries washed away.

One Wedding (As Promised)

Also Shrove Tuesday

REVEREND OSBOURNE WASN'T a dog collar, blazer and slacks kind of vicar. Black jeans were more his thing, accompanied by Converse boots and T-shirts that looked like heavy metal band merch until you got close enough to read the gothic text depicting the Word of the Lord. He was, legit, one of Jesus's biggest fans, and slowly but surely, he was winning over his parishioners…even if some of the older folk were still affronted by his rockin' style.

He wore the dog collar for services, of course, and when he was on official business. That he was wearing it to Henry and Daniel's wedding meant the world, but the twitch he'd developed from fighting the urge to tug it away from his neck had the two grooms on the brink of nervous giggles. At least, Henry was on the brink, and if he went, he'd take Daniel with him. So it had always been.

With the civil (in all meanings of the word, astonishingly) part of the ceremony done, the registrar stepped aside, and Reverend Osbourne moved forward to speak. Henry used the change-around to glance over his shoulder, quickly scanning the rows of guests. Emma—Daniel's twin sister— had been in charge of seating and had put literally months into coming up with the 'least combustible' arrangement.

To that end, Daniel's family—normal, sensible, got along famously—were all seated together, front-left, with his friends and select work colleagues behind, while Henry's clan—like a busload of E-number-high six-year-olds on a school trip—were dotted all over the show with the bakery staff and other friends forming sturdy people barriers between. His mum and Grandma Parker were at one end of the front row; Gran and Grandad Jones were at the other. Two rows behind them was Aunty Jen, along with Nessa's littluns; back another two rows were Aunty Susan, Uncle John and Henry's other cousins.

As for Henry's dad...

He was there, all right, and he'd put himself at the back of the room, though Henry wished more than anything his dad had forgotten or bottled out or whatever stopped him showing up to every previous event to which Henry had invited him. His suit was creased, he wore no tie, and he looked drunk. He always looked drunk, irrespective of whether he was.

A subtle nudge from Daniel reminded Henry where he was and why, and he turned to face front, focusing on Reverend Osbourne's patient smile and doing his best to ignore his almost (they had yet to sign the register) husband's frown.

"Daniel, Henry..." The reverend's smile broadened as he peered down on them for several seconds, then up and over them, at their guests. "Family and friends, it is my privilege to join you on this very special day."

As he did on Sunday mornings, the reverend spoke with clarity and slow deliberation, emphasising certain words—*privilege...special...*

"When Daniel and Henry first came to discuss their wedding with me, I'd been in Banton less than three months. They were the fifth couple with whom I'd met. Alas, they were the first I had to turn away.

"The Church is prevented by law from conducting weddings for people of the same sex, nor do the Bishops permit me to conduct a service of blessing for this wonderful union. But who would doubt the love these two young men share?"

Henry turned to Daniel, quite certain they had matching pink cheeks and silly wide grins.

Reverend Osbourne chuckled and held out his hands. "Love speaks for itself, does it not?"

Murmurs of agreement rumbled around the room like a distant, departing storm. The reverend waited for them to dissipate before he spoke again.

"Daniel and Henry have declared before you that they will live together, bonded by their love. They have made promises to each other and exchanged solemn vows. In a short while, they will formalise their commitment under English law. They have also chosen to mark their commitment to each other with prayer."

Henry and Daniel, still with hands clasped, bowed their heads, and an incredible silence filled the room. Not a whisper was heard, not even from the children.

"Loving and gracious God, who made us in your image and sent your son Jesus Christ to welcome us home; protect us in love and empower us for service. Through the power of the Holy Spirit, may Daniel and Henry become living signs of his love, and may we uphold them in the promises that each make this day, through Jesus Christ our Lord. Amen."

"Amen."

"Jesus told us to 'Love the Lord your God with all your heart, with all your soul, with all your strength and with all your mind' and 'love your neighbour as yourself'. For the love that we receive and give let us all thank God, saying together...

"Almighty God, source of all being, we thank you for your love, which creates and sustains us. We thank you for the physical and emotional expression of that love; and for the blessings of companionship and friendship. We pray that we may use your gifts so that we can ever grow into a deeper understanding of love and of your purpose for us, through Jesus Christ, our Lord. Amen."

"A reading from 1 Corinthians 13, verses one to thirteen:

"I may be able to speak the languages of human beings and even of angels, but if I have no love, my speech is no more than a noisy gong or a clanging bell. I may have the gift of inspired preaching; I may have all knowledge and understand all secrets; I may have all the faith needed to move mountains—but if I have no love, I am nothing. I may give away everything I have, and even give up my body to be burnt—but if I have no love, this does me no good.

"Love is patient and kind; it is not jealous or conceited or proud; love is not ill-mannered or selfish or irritable; love does not keep a record of wrongs; love is not happy with evil, but is happy with the truth. Love never gives up; and its faith, hope, and patience never fail.

"Love is eternal. There are inspired messages, but they are temporary; there are gifts of speaking in strange tongues, but they will cease; there is knowledge, but it will pass. For our gifts of knowledge and of inspired messages are only partial; but when what is perfect comes, then what is partial will disappear.

"When I was a child, my speech, feelings, and thinking were all those of a child; now that I have grown up, I have no more use for childish ways. What we see now is like a dim image in a mirror; then we shall see face to face. What

I know now is only partial; then it will be complete—as complete as God's knowledge of me.

"Meanwhile these three remain: faith, hope, and love; and the greatest of these is love.

"This is the word of the Lord."

"Thanks be to God."

"Daniel and Henry..."

Henry was immediately attentive and returned Daniel's earlier nudge accompanied by a knowing smile. The Scriptures always transported Daniel to some other place, a different level of consciousness. He blinked several times, as if waking from a nap, and mouthed an apology at Henry and the reverend. Henry thought his heart might burst from how much he loved this man.

"Daniel and Henry," Reverend Osbourne repeated, finally securing the attention of both. "Will you be to each other a companion in joy and a comfort in times of trouble, and will you give each other opportunity for love to deepen?"

"We will, with God's help."

"Will you, Daniel, give yourself to Henry, sharing your love and your life, your wholeness and your brokenness, your success and your failure?

"I will."

"Will you, Henry, give yourself to Daniel, sharing your love and your life, your wholeness and your brokenness, your success and your failure?"

"I will."

"Jesus, our brother, inspire Daniel and Henry in their lives together, that they may come to live for one another and serve each other in true humility and kindness. Through their lives may they welcome each other in times of need and in their hearts may they celebrate together in their times of joy, for your name's sake. Amen."

"*Amen.*"

"Let us say together…Our Father, *who art in Heaven…*"

The mass of voices swelled and merged like the balls of dough Henry's grandad used to leave to prove, the resulting bread rolls often bearing tiny dents where naughty Henry had poked his finger. He'd been a little monster, far worse than Nessa's two. But today, he wasn't the poker; he was one of Reverend Osbourne's bread rolls, squishing into Daniel, and when they were baked, nothing would ever tear them apart.

That was marriage. That was baking. That was Henry, daydreaming his way through The Lord's Prayer.

"*…the power and the glory, for ever and ever, Amen.*"

"Spirit of God, you teach us through the example of Jesus that love is the fulfilment of the Law. Help Daniel and Henry to persevere in love, to grow in mutual understanding, and to deepen their trust in each other; that in wisdom, patience and courage, their life together may be a source of happiness to all with whom they share it; and the blessing of God Almighty, Creator, Redeemer and Sustainer be upon you to guide and protect you and all those you love, today and always. Amen."

"*Amen.*"

"Heavenly Father, we are your children, made in your image. Hear our prayer that fathers and mothers, sons and daughters, may find together the perfect love that casts out fear, walk together in the way that leads to eternal life, and grow up together into the full humanity of your Son, Jesus Christ our Lord. Amen."

"*Amen.*"

***

"No apology needed! Thanks so much for coming." Daniel embraced his departing colleague side on. The small fractious baby in her arms screamed louder still.

"Thank you for inviting me. The ceremony was lovely, as was the reception, apart from..." The woman smiled apologetically and rubbed her child's back. "He's colicky."

"Aww, poor mite," Daniel cooed. He liked babies and flat-out *adored* Nessa's kids. They'd have their own someday.

"Now, if the gift's wrong..." the woman began.

"I'm sure it's perfect!"

"I have the receipt if it's not. See you in two weeks."

Henry and Daniel waved as she departed, and Henry rubbed his ear. "That baby could be the next town crier," he said.

Daniel nodded and laughed. A couple of other guests were getting ready to go, but Henry's attention was on Nessa. He'd spotted her at the bar a while ago, and she kept glancing to see if they were free. They were, so she was on her way over. "Hey, cuz," Henry greeted.

"Hey. You two OK for drinks?"

They both nodded and reached for their glasses at the same time. Nessa rolled her eyes.

"Soooo...did you see her?"

"Who?"

"Margaret."

"Where?" Henry made a quick, panicked search of the room.

"Not now, you nutter. After the service. In the foyer?"

"Really? What's she even doing here?"

Nessa shrugged. "There's a Chamber of Commerce meeting this evening. Maybe she's here for that."

"Or she was trying to sneak a peek at our wedding cake..." Henry was ever suspicious of Margaret Sharpe's intentions. He looked over to the top tables, where his mum and grandma were *still* admiring the three-tier white and silver cake, although he'd been as bad. On this occasion, he resisted the temptation to take photos…more photos…of it. They'd only start on him again if he went anywhere near.

***

Henry can dilly-dally all he likes, but at some point soon, he and Daniel will have to make that inaugural cut. After all, what's the point in having their cake and *not* eating it? His reluctance is understandable, though, for it is a stunning creation. True, the icing is patchy in places, and some of those swirls are a bit on the wobbly side, but from a distance, no-one would know. Or no-one but Henry.

Yes, he's stubborn and fussy and often gets worked up over little things he can do nothing about, but he knows his grandad struggled this time, even if he's doing a sterling job of hiding it. And he knows Nessa is worried what will happen to the bakery after Grandad's gone—what if he's left the building to Henry's dad? (It would be disastrous, that's what, but he's not popping his clogs on my watch, so we can safely forget about it for now…or can we?)

Henry also knows this is probably the last wedding cake his grandad will make.

Which is sad.

So sad.

Still, if nothing else, it's something for the village annals:

> *The last 'Henry Jones' wedding cake was made by Henry the Seventh on the occasion of his grandson's marriage to Daniel Miller, which was also Banton's first same-sex marriage.*

***

"You know what? I hope she did see our cake—in fact, I'm going to take her a piece." Henry finished his champagne in one big gulp and handed his glass to Daniel.

"What…you're doing that now?" Nessa's horror was clear to see, but no, he didn't mean right now.

"You can take it round there tomorrow if you like. Come on." Without further ado, Henry marched off, expecting Nessa to follow. She didn't.

"What are you doing?" she called after him, then asked Daniel, "What's he doing?"

"Not sure."

Henry sighed and went back.

Daniel grimaced. "Uh-oh. I know that look."

"She's brought this on herself," Henry said. "Are you coming?" This time, he hooked his arm around Nessa's, and she could easily have pulled away but instead went willingly, more or less.

"You're not going to do something silly, are you?"

"I don't plan to. I had an idea."

"OK?"

"Wedding cakes."

"Whoa." Nessa tugged on his arm, effectively putting on the brakes. "I'm sure we already discussed this. We can't afford to employ another baker."

"But we could if we took on an apprentice."

Nessa's brow creased, but the frown was gone before it fully formed. She was considering it. "Who'll train them? Our bakers are bread specialists—"

Henry nodded slowly, leaving her to figure it out in her own time.

"—and none of us know the first thing about cake decorating. Even if we managed to talk my mum into helping us out more, she can't do fancy cakes. We'd need an artist like Granda…doh."

Henry beamed. "Yes!"

"No, Hen. We'd have to tell him about…" She wiggled her finger between them.

"I know. It's time, Ness."

"Are you insane? It's your wedding day!"

"You were going to tell him after the wedding anyway. I'm actually surprised you haven't told him already."

Nessa shook her head in denial, but she couldn't fool Henry. He'd felt her bristling when Grandad was narrating the bakery's history, like they hadn't heard it a dozen times before, and it always ended the same way—Grandad's guilt for how Henry's dad turned out, with absolutely no acknowledgement of his brilliant daughters, who had succeeded in spite of him.

It wasn't Henry's dad he'd failed, it was Aunty Jen and Aunty Susan, and the only way Henry and Nessa could make him see sense was to prove to him how successful *their* bakery was. So successful, in fact, they'd sold two gross pancakes in under four hours, and that wasn't a one-off. But, of course, Nessa had been set on getting Henry to go home and get ready for his wedding, so she'd let the opportunity pass.

"It's been such a lovely day, Hen. Don't ruin it now."

No need for her to worry on that score.

"Oh, no." Henry closed his eyes, counted to five, and opened them again, whispering to Nessa, "I thought he'd left after the ceremony."

"Apparently not."

(Henry's dad at two o'clock—directionally. Chronologically, it's closer to seven.)

Henry's dad halted but kept his distance.

"Hello, Henry," he said.

"Dad," Henry said.

Awkward shoe-gazing and feet-shuffling ensued, and neither spoke for several seconds. Indeed, their entire relationship may well have ended in goodbyes right then and there, were it not for Nessa's intervention.

"How are you, Uncle Henry? You're looking well."

Henry the younger peeped through his eyelashes and had to agree. Aside from the crumpled suit, his dad seemed healthier—and happier—than ever.

"Yeah?" Henry's dad's smile was so genuine it were as if he'd never smiled before. "Thanks, Vanessa."

"Just Nessa," she corrected. "Or Ness."

"Sorry. I..." He stuffed his hands in his pockets and shrugged, so much like Grandad. "I'm sorry if I offended you."

"You didn't," she assured him, which was a blatant lie. Even when they were arguing, Henry wouldn't dare call her Vanessa. She hated it.

"So...um...Henry?"

Henry nodded and looked up, at once captured by blue eyes too familiar, in his peripheral vision the same brown hair, pointy ears, squodgy noses—his reflection eighteen years into the future.

"Have you enjoyed your day?"

Henry nodded again and found his tongue. "Yes, I have. The happiest of my life."

There was that smile again. "I'm glad. You deserve it."

"Thanks, Dad. I...um...didn't realise you were still here."

"Your sister-in-law's been taking care of me." He glanced around him, a bit shifty-like.

"You escaped, didn't you?" Nessa said with a chuckle.

Henry's dad grimaced and turned pink. "I told her I needed a slash. I mean, I do, and I'll get going soon, but I couldn't leave without speaking to my son." He met Henry's gaze again. "I'd like to meet Daniel at some point, if it's all right with you."

Decision time.

Henry looked over at Daniel—watching them, expression pensive—and then at his grandad—also watching them, pretending he wasn't—and finally at Nessa.

"I'll talk to Grandad," she said.

Henry sighed, part relief, part nervousness, and kissed her cheek. "Thanks, cuz."

She waved him away and strode off, full of confidence and purpose; Henry watched to make sure she safely made it to Grandad (because a hotel function room is a terribly treacherous terrain to traverse) and beckoned to his dad, leading the way back to Daniel, who immediately straightened and fixed a smile over his mild surprise.

"Mr. Jones," he said and extended his hand.

"Mr. Jones?" said Henry's dad, accepting the handshake. "That's my dad. And my dad's dad, and his dad…" He laughed and gave Henry a sideways glance, as anxious as Henry was himself. "My mates call me Jonesy. Would that be weird?"

"Yes," Daniel said. "Yes, it would."

"Right." Henry's dad sucked his teeth and shrugged. "Mr. Jones it is, then. Good to meet you, son-in-law." He put his arm around Henry's shoulders and grinned. "You landed a good'un here, lad. A right chip off the old block."

Daniel eyed Henry in alarm. Somewhere out of line of sight, Aunty Susan muttered—quite loudly, "Chip off the old block? Is he having a laugh?"

Henry's dad's grin drooped, along with his arm. "So, Daniel, what do you do?"

"Job, you mean? I'm a teacher."

"Yeah?"

"Yes…primary school…" Daniel's eyes strayed past Henry and his dad to what was going on behind them. (Short version: The War of The Joneses.) "The local primary school. How about you, Mr. Jones? What do you do?"

"Maintenance technician at the Clayworks."

"Oh, wow." Daniel raised his voice to be heard over the din. "I bet that's interesting." He was just making it up as he went along. "And hard work."

"It can be. I'm on the nightshift—that's the only time the kilns aren't operating, but they're still bloody hot…" Henry's dad fell silent—one of his acid flashbacks, perhaps—while the racket behind them escalated to the point of being impossible to ignore.

With much dread and a fair idea of the sight that would greet him, Henry turned around.

"…just waltzes in here like he didn't destroy this family while you—" Aunty Susan pointed at Grandad accusingly "—welcome him like the prodigal bloody son."

"Sue," Aunty Jen calmly beseeched, but Aunty Susan wasn't done.

"And you're still stuck on it, Dad. After all these years, you still think he's going to change. Be the son you always wanted him to be. Well, I've got news for you…"

"I'll go," Henry's dad said.

"No, Dad."

53

"I'm sorry, son. I shouldn't have come." With a quick hug for Henry and another handshake for Daniel, Henry's dad dodged out of the nearest exit, unseen by the rest of the family.

"Come on, Sue," Jen tried again, still keeping her cool. "This isn't the place for it."

"Isn't it, Jen? Isn't it? One word from that...jackass brother of ours, and *he*—" another vicious jab of the finger at Grandad "—will snatch the bakery right out of Ness and Henry's hands."

"Sue, that's enough!" Jen bellowed. "Come on! We're going for some fresh air." Gripping Susan firmly by the hand, Jen steered her towards and out of the door. It was several seconds later before their argument could no longer be heard.

"Oh God," Henry whispered, not in blasphemy, and buried his face in his hands.

"Well, that was exciting," Daniel said far too gleefully.

"Exciting?"

"Hen, Hen, I'm so sorry."

Henry peered at Nessa through his fingers. "It's OK. It wasn't your fault...was it?"

"No, but..." She sighed so heavily her breath reached Henry's partly shielded eyeballs. "I didn't tell him. I was going to, but he heard your dad and got all uppity."

Henry let his hands drop. "I thought you were the brave one, Ness."

"I am!" she protested, and she was. Growing up in their family, under the benevolent but misguided rule of a patriarch, she'd had to be. She was also thoroughly disappointed with herself.

"Look on the bright side," Henry said, "Aunty Susan's just done the hard bit for us."

"I suppose so," Ness accepted. "And by the time you're back from your honeymoon, he'll be over the shock. Then you can hit him with your wedding cake idea. On which note…"

Henry's mouth fell open, but before he could respond, Nessa whipped her hand from behind her back, dazzling both men with the flash of ten inches of tempered, sharpened steel.

"Gosh, is that a massive knife in your hand, Nessa?" Daniel said.

She grinned. "Nah. I'm always pleased to see you. Shall we?" With a dangerous flourish, she directed them towards their cake, and they went willingly. More or less.

A Bun in the Oven

March

E NGLISH BAKERS HAVE something of a penchant for concocting sweet treats with, if not a distinctive local flavour, names which ensure there can never be any doubt as to the origin of said treat.

The Eccles Cake, for instance, hails from the Greater Manchester town of Eccles, and its slightly older oval cousin, the Banbury Cake, from Banbury, Oxford. Both consist of flaky pastry stuffed (and I do mean stuffed) with currants and generously sprinkled with demerara sugar. They're best eaten cold, really, as they're a bit of a fire risk with all that sugar.

Not dissimilar is the Chorley Cake, except it's flatter, made with shortcrust pastry and no added sugar. Apparently, currants are sweet enough for Chorley folk, hardened Lancastrians that they are.

Then there's the Bakewell Tart—a shortcrust base upon which are layered jam and frangipane topped with flaked almonds or sometimes icing—and the Gloucester Tart, which is made with ground rice rather than frangipane.

It would be terribly remiss of me not to mention the dessert that could be found in every British school canteen in the 1970s and 80s: the Manchester Tart. A pastry base (or cardboard, possibly), a scraping of jam and a slab of custard (vibrant yellow, back in the day) with desiccated coconut just kind of free-floating on top. Honestly, it was delicious—

there was nothing quite so magnificent as arriving at the canteen at lunchtime to discover it was a Manchester Tart day.

Lastly, but by no means leastly, I present for your delight and delectation the Banton Bun, which is neither cake nor tart but something between a scone and a bread roll, which may or may not have had something to do with its creator, one Henry Jones the Fourth, falling asleep one morning while the dough was rising. It rose, and it rose…and it rose some more. And then…

It collapsed.

Poor Henry. He worked so hard. The bakery was bigger, more successful than he or his father could ever have imagined, but it would all be for nothing if, even for a day, the villagers had to do without bread. He was exhausted and could no longer cope on his own; he needed an assistant.

But first, he needed to rescue the dough.

In a heroic effort to 'waste not, want not', he added a cupful of soda to the gloopy mess, gave it a quick knead, put it in the oven and hoped for the best.

Later that morning, Josephine, daughter of farmer Edward Thatcher (yes, indeed) was passing the bakery on her way to the grocery with the milk and butter when her horse spooked, almost toppling the cart and knocking Josephine to the ground.

Upon hearing the commotion, Henry immediately—and fatefully—raced to the aid of the young damsel in distress, and the rest, as we say, is history. And *her*story, of course. After all, were it not for Josephine taking a knife to one of Henry's insubstantial buns (sounds way more gruesome than it was) and sprucing it up with a generous dollop of cherry preserve and whisked cream, the Banton Bun may never have seen the light of day.

"It's not quite there," Henry said, taking another bite of their brand-new creation.

"I think it's delicious," Josephine murmured, licking cream from her lips. Henry blushed as red as the cherry preserve. Josephine shuffled along the bakery bench, closer to Henry. Closer still. Closer... "You know what it needs?" Josephine's lips brushed Henry's cheek. He dumbly shook his head. "It needs..."

She whispered in his ear.

He smiled. He nodded. "Yes!"

And so it was.

One final point: Josephine is Margaret's great-great-great-great-aunt, so yes; she and Henry are distantly related, and she probably has a rightful claim to the Joneses' secret family recipe.

But I'm not going to tell her that. Are you?

***

Henry could wait no longer. Not even long enough to flip the sign to 'closed', although it was late morning—their quiet period, hence it was when Nessa had booked her doctor's appointment—and Henry wouldn't be away more than a couple of minutes.

Typically, the shop bell tinkled the second he'd started to.

"Tough luck," he muttered and got on with it. There were no thieves in Banton. Well, there were, but they tended not to steal from their own, and in any case the few quid in the till wouldn't get them very far. No, whoever it was would wait, and if they couldn't, there was always THE Village Bakery...

With that thought, Henry squeezed, trying to pee faster and cursing that third cup of coffee. "Stick at two in future," he admonished himself as he shook off, zipped, flushed, washed his hands, ignored his panda-face reflection in the tiny mirror over the basin, hurried back to the shop...and stopped like a sheet of glass had slammed down in front of him when he saw who was there.

"Oh! It's you."

Margaret Sharpe. In his bakery. Unattended.

Henry edged along the counter and slid open the cabinet door, smiling like a madman.

"Henry, *what* are you doing?"

Surreptitiously checking for signs of sabotage. "Ensuring I'm ready to serve you, Mrs. Sharpe. What will it be? A slice of lemon drizzle cake? Jam tart, perhaps? I'd offer you a Banton Bun, but, you know..."

"Hmm." She raised her chin, all haughty, but it lasted only a second or two, ending in a sigh, followed by, "How was the wedding?"

"The...w-w-what?"

"I haven't seen you to ask. Did it go well?"

"Yes...thank you...for asking." Henry straightened the paper bags in bewilderment.

"Good, good." Margaret nodded, quite a lot. "And your wedding cake? Was it everything you hoped for?"

"Um...yes, it was." Henry cut to the chase. "Look, Margaret, I appreciate your interest, and I'm not trying to cause a fight, but...did you really come here to ask about our wedding?"

Henry's question wiped the big fake grin from her face, but what replaced it was far worse: a rueful smile. Margaret Sharpe did *not* wear rueful well.

"Ah, Henry, you always were such a perceptive boy."

Man, he corrected in his head but let it slide.

"I popped in to give you this." Margaret unclipped her handbag and pulled out a white envelope. "I had hoped to give it to you on the day." She reached forward, offering it to Henry. "After what passed, it would have seemed disingenuous, so I felt it best to wait."

Perplexed, Henry took the envelope and studied the front, on which was written 'Henry and Daniel'.

"I was uncertain whose surname to use. Traditionally, it would be the husband's, but, well, you understand my dilemma, I'm sure."

"I do," Henry uttered, by now having extracted the card from the envelope and not quite believing his eyes. It was just a generic 'Congratulations on Your Marriage' card, signed with a neutral 'Best wishes, Margaret and Peter Sharpe', but still. It was a wedding card from Margaret Sharpe. "Thank you. This is…lovely."

"My pleasure." She fussed with her coat buttons. "Well, I must—"

"Would you like to see the cake?"

"I'd be delighted!"

***

Approximately fifteen minutes from now, when Nessa returns from her doctor's appointment to find Henry and Margaret enthusing over the *one hundred and twenty-six* photos Henry took of his wedding cake, she'll wonder if gluten intolerance can cause hallucinations. Probably not, but now you know why she's been to the doctor (the gluten intolerance, not the hallucinations—we'll leave those to Henry's dad), and it's going to set the bakery on an entirely new course, but that won't happen until long after we've said goodbye to the lovely people of Banton.

As for what Margaret's up to—the wedding card, the well wishes—yes, it's all a wee bit suspicious. But her intentions are good. *Mostly* good. Bear in mind she wasn't always a baker, although really, who makes their own wedding cake? OK, some people do, but my point is, Margaret didn't. Henry's grandad made it, and it was beautiful. One of his best, without a doubt. Was it *the* best? Margaret likes to think so, and she's only interested in seeing Henry's photos to reassure herself whilst unaware that Henry is sharing them with her for the exact same reason. Who knows, maybe they're both right in their own way.

But that's only a part of the story. The rest has a lot to do with a meeting at the village hall this coming Wednesday, along with a few pointers from Reverend Osbourne on how Margaret might begin to heal the rift with Henry and Daniel. She might never approve of their marriage—the card was the reverend's idea—but she knows better than most that times change, and attitudes change with them. She also knows beyond doubt that Henry and Daniel's love is true, faithful and strong. How could she not when, as a young woman working in her parents' shop, she cooed over those baby boys as if they were her own.

Perhaps this lady is for turning after all.

***

"Jones," Henry said. "We're Henry and Daniel Jones because of..." He circled his finger in the air to indicate the bakery.

"A logical decision," Margaret concurred, "although Daniel's family has excellent standing in the community."

Henry pursed his lips. It was the usual jab at his dad and the shame he'd brought on the Joneses. It wasn't as if Margaret was the only villager who held that view—they all did—but Henry was proud of his family. He refused to deny his heritage.

"And did you have—oh, yes. Look at that." Margaret shifted her glasses down her nose to inspect the photo more closely. "Two little grooms."

"Yes," Henry confirmed, his thoughts spinning ahead to the sourcing of suitable cake toppers for their wedding cakes, assuming there would be wedding cakes, seeing as Grandad was still 'thinking about it'. Henry was in half a mind to ask where Margaret got hers, but Nessa arrived before the other half of his mind caught up.

"Hey, Hen, guess….wh… Margaret?" She stumbled to a stop before she reached the counter.

"Good morning, Nessa, dear. How are you?"

"I'm…fine? I think?" Her eyes shifted from Margaret to Henry, to the wedding photos, and back to Henry.

"Margaret popped in with a card," he explained.

"O…K. I, um…" Nessa shook her head rapidly and blinked a few times. Henry stifled a laugh. She was right to be confused. He was feeling that way himself. "I'm gonna go… do something," she said, scooting past them to the kitchen, and there she stayed until Margaret left the premises.

"You two were getting on surprisingly well," were Nessa's first words upon her return. It sounded like an accusation, and Henry was fairly sure it was.

"I was just showing her the wedding cake."

"Uh-huh? I hope you didn't leave her unattended."

"Er, well…" Henry shut one eye in a grimace. "Not exactly. But she didn't poke her nose anywhere she shouldn't."

"Hen…"

"I know, I'm sorry! I drank too much coffee this morning, and—"

"Lock the door next time."

"Yes, sorry. I will." He dodged into his seat and hid behind his computer. If he couldn't see her…

Nessa grunted. "Did she tell you about the environmental health?"

"No?"

"Oooooh…gossip time!" She perched on Henry's desk, her disgruntlement forgotten. "Someone told the council they found mouse droppings in their seeded batch."

"Now that's what you call an eye for detail," Henry joked, though he was terrified of mice, especially if they were only three doors down the high street. "So that's why she was here—she's been shut down?"

"Nope. The environmental health inspector found no evidence of mice, but the word on the street is Margaret's confidence has taken a beating."

"The word on the street? Did you turn gangsta while I was on my honeymoon, cuz?"

Nessa ignored his mockery. "You know what this means? Someone's trying to stop Banton taking part in the County Cake-Off."

"Don't be ridiculous, Ness. It's only a stupid baking contest."

"It's a big deal, Hen. Cash prizes, loads of publicity, kudos—there's a whisper one of the TV networks is interested in it."

"Pshure. As if they're gonna bother with a few Victoria sponge cakes at the county fair."

"Reality TV's all the rage, Hen. Sooooo, anyway…" Nessa unhooked a mug from the tree, filled it with coffee and offered it to Henry. He waved it away. "Are you coming to the meeting on Wednesday?"

"Meeting?"

"To figure out what we're doing for the Cake-Off."

"Why are you even asking me that?"

"Just checking you hadn't changed your mind."

"Not a chance."

***

Wednesday evening

"That's it, I'm done." Daniel slapped his planner shut and shoved it back in his bag. "I can't concentrate with all your fussing and fidgeting."

"Sorry." Henry's phone vibrated across the table. He unlocked it and fake-sobbed as he read the message onscreen.

"What does she want this time?"

"Who?"

"Nessa?" Daniel moved over to the sofa and switched on the TV. "It *is* Nessa, isn't it?"

"Yeah." Henry went to join him. He didn't even get his bottom on the seat before his phone vibrated again.

"Just turn it off," Daniel advised.

"I can't."

"Why not?"

"Because…" He trailed off as he read the message.

> *Please Hen. The hot Rev. Ozzy says we need something spectacular. Suggestions?*

"Because?" Daniel repeated.

Henry sighed. "Because I can't."

***

There it is again, that familiar obstinate streak. Chop any Henry Jones in half—hypothetically speaking—and he'd have lettering running right through him like a stick of rock:

One Stubborn Bugger

Herein lies the problem. Since Nessa told him about the notice in the village hall, Henry's stuck to his guns. He's not doing the Cake-Off. Absolutely not. No way, José.
Except
he really,
really,
really,
wants to do
the Cake-Off.

***

He called her back.
"Is Margaret there?"
"What kind of question is that?"
Henry got up and started pacing. "Put her on, Ness."
"Wh—"
"I've got an idea. Quick!"
"OK, OK, hold on."
After a half-minute of muffled scuffling, Margaret's (not surprisingly) surprised voice sounded at the other end. "Hello?"
"Margaret, it's Henry. What's the biggest Banton Bun you've ever made?"
"Hmm…about eight inches. Why?"
"Could you make bigger?"
"Of course."

"How much bigger?"

"How big are you thinking?"

"The size of a Mini."

"The size of a Mini?" Margaret squeaked. "Why would you...oh! Yes, well, that would be rather spectacular, wouldn't it?"

"Yes." Henry was nodding along and grinning, and Daniel was shaking his head at him like he was completely bonkers. Daniel flapped his hand, and Henry moved out of the way of the TV. "Could we do it?" he asked Margaret.

"Theoretically, if we had a large enough oven."

"Would ours be large enough?" Theirs was the oven Henry's grandad had installed, back when the bakery employed thirteen members of staff.

"We'd get the dough in," Margaret confirmed. "But once it starts to rise..."

Henry smacked his forehead at his oversight. Rubbish baker that he was, he still knew dough doubled its size. "OK, how big does this oven need to be?"

"Well, big enough to fit a Mini inside. Or half a Mini, at least—we'd have to bake the two halves separately."

"That's a bit more manageable." Who was he kidding? "What about a pizza oven? The pizza restaurant in town might help us out."

"I doubt theirs is any bigger than yours."

"OK..." Henry clutched wildly at straws. "Could we barbecue it?"

Daniel snorted at something on TV, or Henry thought that was what he was snorting at until he realised the news was on—not even an 'And finally...' witty ditty. Daniel was laughing at him.

Henry glared, and Daniel attempted to straighten his face, but a residual smirk of amusement remained.

"Never mind, Henry," Margaret consoled. "I'm sure we'll come up with something just as spectacular but...possible. Perhaps aim for quantity? If we use both kitchens, we could bake an awful lot of normal-sized Banton Buns in seventy-two hours."

"OK, Margaret," Henry agreed tightly. "Whatever you think is best." With a huff, he hung up on her and stared, unseeing, at the TV. "I hate admitting defeat."

"I know you do," Daniel said.

"This is why I tried not to get involved. I mean, it's just a stupid baking contest."

"Yes."

"It's not important."

"No."

Henry re-joined Daniel on the sofa and tuned in to the newsreader's drone. He heard about three words before his mind took off again, imagining trestle tables lined with hundreds of Banton Buns. Impressive, yes, but was it spectacular?

"There's got to be a way," he mused aloud.

"There is," Daniel said without taking his eyes off the TV. Henry swivelled to face him. "There is?"

"Your dad."

"My dad?" Henry scoffed. "He's got even less clue about baking than I have, unless we're planning to get the judges stoned on hash cakes."

"That wasn't what I meant, Hen. He works the nightshift at the Clayworks."

"How's that supposed to...ohhhhh." The penny dropped. "He works the nightshift at the Clayworks."

"Yep"

"And kilns are *massive* ovens." Henry grabbed Daniel's head with both hands and planted a sloppy kiss somewhere in the face region. "You're a genius," he said. He jumped up from the sofa and sprinted from the room. "I'll call him on the way."

"Way where?"

"The village hall. Don't wait up!"

May Day, May Day

Not Quite May Day

County Show Cake-Off
Rules of Entry:

1. One entry per village.

2. All those involved must reside in said village at the time of the contest.

3. Entries must be prepared a maximum of seventy-two hours before judging takes place and must be entirely edible.

4. All entries and entrants will present to the County Fair main marquee at twelve noon on May Day.

5. Any entrants breaking the rules above will be immediately disqualified from the contest.

***

"The oven is all well and good," said Margaret, "but where on earth will we get an oven tray to fit it?"

All eyes were on Henry, and he racked his brains, searching out solutions. Short of growing a magic beanstalk...

"I ask my boss man," said Igor—the scary-looking trucker who lived in his cab and parked up at the back of the church in between jobs, with Reverend Osbourne's permission. "He gets things done."

Henry doubted, but the reverend's faith overruled.

"Thank you, Igor. Keep me posted."

The gigantic trucker gave a singular nod, and the meeting moved on.

Don't make problems, create solutions. It seemed to be Reverend Osbourne's philosophy too, and Henry was in awe. By the end of the evening, everyone was on board—

"I'm delighted you've joined us, Henry," the reverend said as they stacked away the chairs. "We couldn't do this without you."

—yes, even Henry.

***

You will need:

- Forklift truck
- Heavy goods vehicle
- Cement mixer
- Teflon-coated aluminium pallet (custom-made)
- Industrial kiln

- 450 lbs strong white flour
- 9 lbs salt
- 8 lbs yeast
- 4 lbs bicarbonate of soda
- 53 gallons buttermilk
- 50 lbs cherry preserve
- 5 gallons cream, whipped
- [redacted]

"What have you got there?" Margaret glanced up from her bucket of yeast and eyed the plain white drum in Henry's arms.

"Oh, just...um..."

"None of your beeswax." Nessa stepped in front of him, blocking Margaret's view.

"Have it your way, dears," Margaret said blithely. "I have *no* interest in your family's *silly* secret ingredient. However, we *are* all in this together. What would Reverend Osbourne have to say?"

"We don't care," Henry muttered as he and Nessa side-stepped together out of the kitchen into the yard—

"I care," Nessa said.

—where the cement mixer merrily churned away under Grandad's supervision.

"You could always invite him round for dinner sometime," Henry suggested. He set the drum on the ground in front of the mixer and levered off the lid. "How much, Grandad?"

"A pound and a half to fifty pounds of flour."

"So...thirteen and a half pounds, but this is only a fifth of the mix." Henry calculated the necessary proportion and added it to the mixer. Maths, he could do. "OK. Nessa, can you stick this back in the safe for now, please."

"Righteo." She scooped up the drum and paused. "Do you think I should? Invite Reverend Osbourne round?"

"Why not? It works for Mrs. Broughton." Henry grinned.

Nessa flicked his ear and marched off with the drum, back through the kitchen whence Henry heard Margaret exclaim to herself, "They keep it in the safe? Honest to goodness!" He ignored her and inspected his checklist.

"OK, where are we up to? Dough...in progress." He'd left that to Grandad and Margaret—the experts. "Transport...jet-washed and ready to go." Courtesy of Igor the Horrible. "Preserve..." He took out his phone. "Aunty Jen, it's Henry. How's the jam coming along?"

"Cooling as I speak."

"Great work!" *Tick.*

That was the other thing Henry could do. He might be a rubbish baker, but when it came to organising people and coordinating who needed to do what and when, he was pretty darn good at it, even if he did think so himself.

Nessa came back out and stood next to him. "Time check."

"Quarter past four." Still sixty-eight hours left. Forty-eight would have sufficed, but the saboteurs hadn't stopped at reporting THE Bakery to the council; they'd done the same to Henry and Nessa, and the environmental health officer was sympathetic, but she had a job to do. Thankfully, like Margaret's, their bakery was given a clean bill of health. Then, the following morning, Henry arrived to find the egg delivery was nothing more than an enormous raw omelette running into the gutter.

That wasn't the end of it. The stopcock on the mains water supply for the entire high street mysteriously turned itself off, Margaret's alarm developed a fault, and then someone threw a firework into the yard. It was at that point Henry called the police, and of course they initially assumed his dad was the culprit. Once Henry and Margaret had given full statements—and Reverend Osbourne had put in a good word for Henry's dad—they released him.

For whatever reason, the vandals hadn't come back after that, but the Banton competitors were taking no chances. At six p.m., accompanied by Henry and Margaret, Igor would transport the dough to the Clayworks, where it was warmer and—Henry was reliably informed—it would speed up the rise. By midnight, the kiln should've cooled to around

150 Celsius, and the baking would commence—under the constant supervision of one of their twenty-strong team.

The Banton Bunnies.

Daniel's contribution. Not a bad one.

And tomorrow, they'd do it all over again with the other half.

***

And the day after that, too, as it turns out.

"But you can't have three halves," I hear you say.

No, indeed you cannot.

***

Seven o'clock, Saturday morning

The door to the foreman's booth opened, startling Henry, who was alert and attentive but entirely focused on the view of the kiln through the grotty heat-retardant window.

"Morning, Margaret." He stretched his arms in the air and stifled a yawn.

She sniffed.

"What's up?"

And sniffed again. "Can you smell that?"

Henry shook his head. "I can't smell anything." Nor could he feel his bottom. The foreman's chair had been comfy two hours ago; now, not so much, but no matter. Margaret was here to take over, and the first half of the bun should be more or less done.

She pointed to the monitor screen on the desk. "Does that work?"

"Yeah. I switched it to standby."

"Henry! You're supposed to be watching our bun."

"Half a bun," he corrected. "And I'm not, I'm watching the oven to make sure no-one tampers with it. What's the point in me watching the bun when I have no idea if it's cooked?" He got up and switched the monitor on, taking the opportunity for a proper stretch. *Home, quick shower, maybe a nap, and back to the bakery—*

Margaret gasped. "Henry! It's burning!" She flapped her hands around in panic.

"Oh heck!"

The two of them dashed from the booth and down the rattly metal stairs to ground level where Henry caught a whiff of burnt toast.

Not burnt toast.

"Open the door," Margaret ordered. "Quick!"

"I'm quicking!" Henry ran over and heaved on the lever, releasing the door lock. "I'll fetch my dad." He dashed off before Margaret got a look at the oven's contents.

A minute later, he was back with his dad and the forklift truck. While Henry senior manoeuvred into position, Henry junior tried to console a devastated Margaret.

"Vehicle reversing, stand clear," the forklift informed them.

Henry steered Margaret out of the way, and the forklift, complete with a five-foot half-sphere of steaming baked produce, emerged from the kiln.

"Well, it's not *burnt* burnt," Henry said, which was true. The half a bun had risen beautifully, but it had a seriously dark crust.

"I...I don't understand," Margaret whimpered. "The temperature is exactly right, the ingredients, the mixing... I've made hundreds...*thousands* of Banton Buns. I did everything exactly the same as always!"

Except...

"Oh...crêpes!" Henry slumped. "I think...this might be...um...our fault."

"What do you mean? Whose fault?" She turned and glared at him. He shrank a little. "What did you do?" she accused.

"OK, well...um...see. I mean, I might be wrong, but—"

"It's your secret ingredient, isn't it?"

Henry pursed his lips.

"What is it?" Margaret demanded.

"I can't tell you."

"So help me. The contest is in two days and we've got to start from scratch! You have to tell me!"

"Please, Margaret, don't make me—"

"Now, Henry!"

"Vanilla sugar," he blurted and clapped his hand over his mouth.

"Sugar?" Margaret screeched. "You added sugar to my recipe?"

"*Your* recipe? Since when?"

"I've been making the Banton Bun for thirteen years!"

"So? My family made it for over a hundred!"

"Henry Jones *and Son*, Baker. Sugar..."

"I didn't think it would matter."

"It's sugar. You add sugar, of course it'll burn, you stupid boy!"

"Excuse me." Henry's dad raised his hand, but they argued over him.

"I'm not a boy, Margaret. I'm twenty-four years old."

"But you accept you're stupid."

"Yes, I'm stupid," Henry snapped. "For ever thinking we could do this together, you...you horrible old bag!"

"Excuse me, folks," Henry's dad tried again. Still no joy.

"That's right, call me names. I came to make peace with you, remember?"

"No, you didn't! You came snooping for the secret ingredient to the *real* Banton Bun!"

"And it's cost us our chance of victory in the County—"

A shrill whistle cut Margaret off mid-flow. Both she and Henry turned and glowered at the source.

Henry's dad laughed in disbelief. "And people say I'm off my bonce? Thank God I went off the rails is all I can say. What do you want me to do with this bread boulder?"

"Chuck it in the skip," Henry said and stormed off up the stairs. He was hot and tired, and sick of everything to do with the Cake-Off. He just wanted to go home.

"Vehicle reversing, stand clear. Vehicle reversing, stand clear..."

"No!" Margaret yelled. "Wait, wait!"

The forklift warning stopped. Curious, Henry stopped too.

"Only the outside is burnt. The inside will still be edible. It would be a terrible waste to throw it away. Couldn't we give it to The Poor?"

Henry about-turned and strolled, hands in pockets, back down the stairs. "You know it's 2018, don't you, Margaret?"

"There are still poor people in 2018, Henry."

"But we don't call them 'The Poor'—"

"What about the soup kitchen in town?" Henry's dad interjected. "They usually only accept non-perishables, but it's got to be worth a shot."

Henry shrugged. Margaret nodded.

"Great. I'll borrow one of the vans and take it down there when I get off shift. For now, I'll stick it in the storeroom." He climbed back onto the forklift.

"Thanks, Dad." Granted, it was an afterthought, but Henry meant it.

"Yes, thank you, Mr. Jones," Margaret added.

Henry's dad gave them a nod, finished reversing his truck and trundled away.

"I'm sorry, Margaret."

"I'm sorry too, Henry."

"What are we going to do?"

"Fix it, dear Henry."

He managed a laugh at that. "How?"

"Pool our resources. Empty our pantries, beg, steal and borrow if we have to…"

***

And that was precisely what they did, apart from the stealing; there was no need. Villagers flocked to the bakery with grocery bags full of flour and salt mined from their pantries. Henry and Nessa traipsed around the farms, buying all the buttermilk available; Grandad made up the shortfall with milk and lemon juice, and Margaret recalculated the cooking time, taking into account the vanilla sugar.

Saturday evening, Igor transported the second enormous ball of dough to the Clayworks to rise; at ten p.m., Henry's dad transferred it to the kiln. Meanwhile, Henry and Nessa were entrusted with mixing the dough for the second half— their first real attempt at baking—so it would be ready to go in the oven at three a.m., by which time the first half should be cooked. If it wasn't, they'd have to leave the second half until Sunday night, and it wouldn't cool in time for the contest. They were flying on a wing and a prayer, and they were exhausted. But they were determined.

Three a.m. Sunday morning, Margaret arrived at the Clayworks with a fencing foil and laughed off the jokes about how rough the village was these days.

"Mr. Jones, when you're ready."

Henry's dad dutifully lifted their creation from the kiln. No burnt-toast smell this time; it was plump, round and golden-brown, and it smelled utterly divine.

"The moment of truth," Margaret said, advancing, foil at the ready. Delicately piercing the soft crust, she plunged the foil deep into the five-foot-wide half-bun, waited a few seconds...and withdrew it. Cheers echoed off the Clayworks' old brick walls when the foil came away clean.

***

By Sunday evening, the two halves were safely stowed in the bakery kitchen where they could slowly cool to room temperature, and the Banton Bunnies gathered in the yard to celebrate with a barbecue and a few drinks.

Henry tapped the barbecue tongs against his beer bottle, garnering everyone's attention. "Reverend Osbourne would like to say a few words."

"Thanks, Henry." The reverend moved so everyone could see him and gave them a moment to read his T-shirt: *And know that I am with you always; yes, to the end of time.* "Well, folks, you really rose to the challenge." That earned him a communal groan. "I'll keep this short because all I want to say is I never doubted for a second we'd succeed, and we have. Whether we win tomorrow is of no consequence, although...it would be nice, wouldn't it?"

"Yes!" came the resounding reply.

"Many, many thanks to all of you for your incredible hard work. Eat, drink, be merry, and get a good night's rest."

All's Fair...

Actual May Day
(or the bank holiday created in its likeness)

WOW!" DANIEL WALKED the circumference of the assembled Banton Bun—twice—and said it again. "Wow!"

"Is that a good wow or a bad wow?" Henry fished. He was a nervous wreck, and Margaret—on the far side of the bun and jabbering at Mr. Sharpe—was in much the same state.

Daniel rolled his eyes, exasperated yet patient; being a primary school teacher had a lot to do with that. "A good wow. It's brilliant, Henry, as are you."

"There's no I in team," Henry blustered and blushed, although it was true he couldn't have done it alone. Well, he couldn't have done it at all, but he was going to change that...just as soon as this contest was out of the way. He sneaked another harried peek at Hillview village's entry on the table next to theirs: shortbread dominoes arranged to depict the village's coat of arms, which was innovative and clever but taking an age to set up when the tiniest jolt from an unsteady hand felled the entire display. Of course, that was what it was supposed to do, but not until the judges were there to see it.

"We should take a look around the fair before it gets too hot," Daniel suggested.

"Can't." Henry stubbornly crossed his arms. "And it's already too hot." He shuddered at the mental image of the judges tucking into their bun, all joyous in their anticipation, and then spitting out the sour cream in disgust.

"But it's cooler outside. Come on, Hen… No-one's going to chance getting up to shenanigans today."

"Better safe than— Oops!"

There went the shortbread dominoes again.

"Pssst, Henry," Margaret whispered, although she was so loud as to make the whispering pointless. She beckoned then changed her mind and came to him, leaning close and cupping her hand around her mouth. "It's her," she said.

Shifting eyes only, Henry looked around their fellow competitors, or those present; of the five villages that had entered the Cake-Off, three had turned up so far, but it was only ten in the morning.

"Who?" he asked.

Margaret shuffled sideways and tapped her shoulder to indicate. "Her."

Henry watched the woman in question apologising to the Hillview competitors for 'accidentally' knocking their table. He didn't recognise her. "Who is she?"

"I don't know, but I'm almost certain she came into the shop the day before the—" Margaret mouthed the words "— mouse droppings incident."

"Guess I was wrong, then." Daniel sighed despondently. "I'll see if I can find us a cup of tea somewhere and come back, OK?"

"There's no point in us all staying," Henry said. "Why don't you go and find Ness? She'll be over by the funfair."

"Why don't you *both* go?" Margaret suggested. "We're fine here, aren't we, Peter?" Mr. Sharpe gave a thumbs up.

"I'd rather hoped to watch the dog agility at eleven, but our bun is more important."

"Then we'll be back for eleven," Henry confirmed.

"If you're sure…"

"It's only fair."

Margaret laughed ruefully. "There is nothing fair about this contest. Now, off you go, boys. Have fun." She shooed them away.

Daniel was right; it was cooler outside, and they wandered through the crowds, at various points being intercepted by children from Daniel's class, excited and surprised to see their teacher.

"We live in the stock cupboards, don't you know," he joked to Henry after one little girl asked if he'd get in trouble for being out of school.

Henry laughed half-heartedly, struggling to get into the spirit of the day in spite of the fun going on all around the park—the rhythmic tinkle of the morris dancers' bells, children singing as they skipped and weaved around the maypole, collies yapping as they warmed up on the agility course—none of it could shake his bad feeling about the Cake-Off.

"Your dad's over there."

"Where?" Henry shielded his eyes from the low morning sun and looked where Daniel was pointing. "Is that woman juggling…"

"Fire, yes," Daniel confirmed, and Henry's dad was at the front of the crowd gathered around the juggler. Indeed, he was standing so close, he'd be lucky to escape unscorched. "Maybe it's as well he didn't take on the bakery, huh?"

"Yes, just as well," Henry agreed. His dad had an unhealthy interest in fire—not exactly a secret—although, after three days of baking, Henry was starting to understand the fascination, not with fire as such; with its magical ability to transform matter. "I think it must run in the family."

Daniel raised an eyebrow but didn't get as far as passing comment, distracted by Nessa, who was waving frantically at them from the top of the Ferris wheel, which she wasn't riding alone. "Well, well, well!"

"Have you seen today's T-shirt?" Henry asked.

"No? What does it say?"

"I am the bread of life."

"Ah, a nice bit of subliminal messaging. Way to go, Rev! He must have loads of T-shirts."

"Yeah. I don't think I've ever seen him wearing the same one twice."

They continued their chatter as they walked around the stalls, indulging in doughnuts and ice cream because it was the done thing. While Henry welcomed the distraction, eleven o'clock couldn't come soon enough, not that he doubted Margaret's valour when it came to protecting their pride and joy.

When they returned to the marquee to take their turn, Henry wasn't in the least surprised to discover the two other competitors still hadn't arrived, and by quarter to twelve it was clear they weren't coming. Whoever had gone after the Banton Bunnies had also frightened off the others, which left just two suspects: Hillview with their shortbread dominoes, and Westleigh with their...Henry had no idea what it was.

"What actually is that?"

"A cupcake replica of Westleigh."

"Right." Henry nodded. It was very colourful and pretty, but it looked nothing like Westleigh village. To Henry's mind, the contest was a two-horse race between Banton and

Hillview, and he honestly didn't care who won as long as it wasn't Westleigh because by now he was almost certain they were the saboteurs.

"All competitors please vacate the marquee. Judging will commence in five minutes." The order was issued by a stout, red-faced man in a tweed blazer to which was pinned a rosette bearing the words 'chief judge'.

With one last check that all was well with their bun, Henry and Daniel left and went to watch the rest of the dog agility display with Margaret and Mr. Sharpe. Now they just had to wait.

***

"Disqualified?" Margaret marched over and yanked out the cardboard sign skewered to their bun. "For what reason?"

"I'm afraid, madam, you broke the rules."

"We did not! We followed them to the letter."

"Mrs. Sharpe...it is Mrs. Sharpe, isn't it?"

"Yes."

"Mrs. Sharpe, is this a cake?"

"Of course it's not, you silly man! It's a Banton Bun."

"Which is a kind of bread, is it not?"

"It's a dessert."

"As that may be, it states clearly in the rules that exhibits must be cake-based."

"Where?" Henry asked. He stepped forward to stand at Margaret's side. "Where in the rules does it say that?"

The chief judge cleared his throat. "Mrs. Tomkins? Would you be so kind..." He held out his hand expectantly, and a timid-looking woman scurried over with a clipboard. "Thank you. Right, let's see..." The man dabbed a handkerchief at his suddenly sweaty neck. "Ah, yes, here we are. Types of desserts to be entered: cakes, biscuits and cookies, brownies and pies. Strictly no breads or products requiring refrigeration."

"Rubbish!" Henry said. "That wasn't in the rules. I'd have seen it if it was."

"And you are?"

"Henry Jones."

"Ah, the famous Henry Jones and Son, Baker, inventor of the Banton Bun—which is not a cake. Now, if you'll excuse me—"

"I will make a formal complaint," Margaret warned. "That rule was added after we entered the contest."

The judge tried to stare her down. "Prove it," he challenged.

Without a word, Henry took out his phone and loaded the PDF of the rules he'd downloaded the night of the meeting at the village hall. "There," he said and thrust it at the obnoxious judge, who barely looked at it.

"Well, it's obvious what's happened here."

"Yes," Henry said. "It's called *cheating*."

The judge laughed, but he'd been caught out and he knew it. "Clearly, you doctored those rules so you could make this…monstrosity. I've made my decision." He turned his back on them.

"Monstrosity?" Margaret repeated, her voice rising in both pitch and volume. In spite of the urge to flee, Henry stayed put. They were a team, after all.

"Mrs. Sharpe, please be quiet or I'll have you removed—"

"*Monstrosity?!*"

"*Mrs. Sharpe!*"

"*How dare you!* Taking bribes from those people with their ridiculous cupcake village. It's an absolute disgrace!"

There was nothing Henry could've done to stop what happened next. Margaret scooped a handful of cream from the middle of their bun and launched it at the judge. Stunned, the man stood still as a statue as whipped cream slid down his face and plopped from his glasses and chin onto his blazer.

Margaret was only just getting started, and she had an impressive aim. Four handfuls fired in quick succession found the woman from Westleigh and her three teammates, while the rest of the Banton Bunnies watched on, astounded, amused, amazed. As Margaret loaded up to take another shot, Henry finally snapped out of his trance.

"Stop!" he yelled and leapt between her and her target, with predictable consequence. The cream thudded against Henry's chest, splattering his face. "Margaret, what are you—"

"Out of my way, Henry!" She re-armed.

"No!" He ducked and blindly grabbed for her, but she broke free and flung the cream with an overarm shot. This time, she missed, or perhaps she didn't, because she got Henry's grandad who'd only come to see what all the commotion was about. Henry stared at his grandad in horror. He had no idea how everything had got out of hand so quickly.

"Agh! I'm hit!" Margaret cried.

Beyond bewildered, Henry spun on the spot and gasped at the sight. A cupcake was stuck to Margaret's cheek, her face twisted in a disgusted sneer as she peeled the cake from her skin, leaving behind a swirly mess of pink and blue glittery buttercream.

Thwack! Something hit Henry on the back of the head, and he stumbled forward into Margaret, who made helicopter arms as she lost her balance and toppled helplessly into the bun. The top half skated eighteen inches backwards, leaving her sitting on a ledge of cream and jam.

"H-hen-ry?" She was shaking with rage.

"Yes, Margaret?" he asked as if steeling himself to hear her dying wish.

"This. Is. War!" On those words, she struggled and wriggled but couldn't quite get traction and made a wild grab for Henry, who momentarily froze. Margaret was furious beyond the capacity for reason, and while Henry wanted revenge as much as the next Bantonion, he was thinking it might be safer to leave her where she was…until Daniel took a cupcake to the chest.

"My favourite shirt!" he cried and crumpled against the marquee's flimsy canvas wall.

That was it. Henry saw red.

Red velvet.

And it was going to stain something chronic.

"I'm with you, Margaret—bakers in arms!"

Determination renewed, Henry grasped her hand and pulled her clear of the bun. Nessa and Reverend Osbourne upended the top half to use as a shield, and every Banton Bunny loaded up with ammunition.

"Aim…" Margaret commanded.

All raised their arms.

"Fire!" Henry and Margaret yelled in unison, and handfuls of whipped cream flew through the air, some finding their targets, most not. Accuracy was difficult under a bombardment of multicoloured cupcakes.

"We're almost out of ammo!" Nessa cried, scraping through to the cherry preserve. It would make a ghastly mess of the marquee, although it was far too late to worry about that.

"Henry, look! He's escaping!" Margaret pointed at the chief judge, who was attempting to crawl, unseen, under the tables.

Henry broke away from the frontline and tore a chunk from the bun. A cupcake whistled past his ear and detonated on impact with Nessa's shield. With Banton Bunnies taking hits all around and buttercream in his hair, Henry bravely struggled on, using the bread to scoop up all that was left of the cream and jam. He turned back to Margaret. "You'll need to cut him off at the overpass," he said.

She nodded her understanding and took the bread, dodging behind their demolished fortress before she went undertable. Cupcake fire was sporadic, the enemy also having depleted their stockpile and caught unawares by shortbread snipers.

In the final throes of battle, everything rested on their last stand, but Margaret was nowhere to be seen, and the chief judge had made it to the end of the marquee. Everything went slow-mo as the man struggled to his feet, and Henry prepared to surrender. Then, as the judge made a run for the door, out of nowhere, Margaret leapt in front of him and smushed the creamy, jammy, soft-with-delicate-hints-of-vanilla bread in his face.

"THAT'S IT!" he roared. "BANTON IS PERMANENTLY BANNED FROM ENTERING THE COUNTY CAKE-OFF!"

"And Westleigh?" Henry demanded. "You're banning them too, yes?"

The judge snorted on each inhale and for a moment looked like he was going to explode (as if things weren't messy enough already). He clenched his fists, his flared nostrils in amid all that cream looking awfully like weeholes in the snow, and gritted out, "The county council *will* hear about this. And you *will* be invoiced for the damage." With that, he marched out of the marquee without looking back.

The Westleigh competitors huddled and jumped up and down, singing, "We are the champions…"

"Oh, poo to you," Henry muttered, turning to his fellow Bantonions. "Who cares about a stupid Cake-Off anyway? We took part. That's what matters."

"On the contrary, dear boy," Margaret said, making it back to them and looking ever so pleased with herself if not a little sullied by assorted confectionery. "Winning is what matters." Anticipating Henry's protest, she raised her voice and went on, "To wit, the Guinness Book of Records will be in touch to arrange a visit."

Henry groaned. "Does that mean we've got to do it all over again?"

"Yes, but it will be bigger, better…"

"Strong and stable," Nessa added. The Banton Bunnies fell about laughing.

"What was that, dear?" Margaret asked, but no-one was listening to her; they were listening to the tannoy announcement:

"The winner of this year's Cake-Off is Westleigh village!"

The Westleigh team cheered loudly and trooped out of the marquee to go and collect their prize.

"So much for TV networks," Nessa grunted. "I can't believe we're banned and *they're* not."

The Hillview team members were nodding in agreement. "If it's any consolation," one of the women said, "we won't be entering next year. Not after all that's gone on. And for the record, we think you should've won. Your Banton Bun was fantastic." She smiled and came over a little dreamy. "I haven't had one in years. My mum used to pick them up whenever she went over to Banton. But the last one I had...I don't know... Nothing tastes quite as good as you remember, does it?"

Henry and Margaret exchanged a knowing glance, and Henry's tummy did a flip. The Joneses didn't yet know he'd let their secret slip.

"Mum's the word," Margaret whispered and tapped the side of her nose.

Half-Day Closing

The Following Wednesday

THE SHOP BELL tinkled, and Henry glanced up. "Hello, you!" he greeted Daniel with a smile and a modicum of surprise. "What are you doing out of school? You'll get a detention."

Daniel laughed. "I've got a permission slip." He came around to Henry's side of the counter. "Reverend Osbourne took assembly this morning and I gave him a lift back to the church."

"Just so you could steal our profit margin?"

"Not *just* for that reason, although I am a bit peckish." He opened the cake cabinet. "Mmm...what do I fancy?"

"Ahem," Henry said and gestured to himself.

Daniel grinned. "Goes without—whoa!" He did a double-take. "Those are Banton Buns."

"Yep." Henry chuckled at Daniel's confused frown. "I'll explain when I get home. On which note, I might be a bit late. I need to finish this business plan."

"OK. I'll make a start on dinner, then." Daniel picked out a bun and took a bite, pondering as he chewed. "Where's Ness?"

"Out back, overseeing a delivery. D'you need to speak to her?"

"I will at some point, but that wasn't why I asked."

"Oh?"

"I think you might get a visit from the reverend this morning."

"He's coming to see Ness?"

"Uh-huh. Anyway, I'd better get back. Morning playtime's nearly over." Daniel moved to leave, but Henry blocked his exit.

"Hold on, you said you didn't come *just* to steal my buns."

Daniel's grin returned, and it was a bit wicked, but he relented at Henry's huff. "OK, you know how, when we were on our honeymoon, you were stressed out about your dad and the Cake-Off and whatnot?"

"Hmm?"

"And you know how teachers get all that time off in the summer?"

"Yes?" Henry folded his arms. The build-up was suspicious.

"Well, Moira the teaching assistant has a villa in Italy."

"Right?"

"And it's available for two weeks in August."

"OK?"

"Hen, are you really going to make me spell this out?"

"You're suggesting we go on holiday."

"I am," Daniel confirmed.

"A summer holiday."

"Correct."

"Hmm." Henry rubbed his chin in a pretence of consideration just long enough to secure a glimpse of Daniel's best puppy-dog-pleading face before he said, "Yes. I'd love to."

"Fantastic!" Daniel hugged him, planted a quick, jam-and-creamy kiss almost on his lips—"See you at home"—

and verily danced, whistling 'Summer Holiday', all the way across the shop.

"Bye," Henry called after him in bemusement. The bell tinkled as the door clicked shut.

Smiling to himself, Henry gave his face a quick wipe with a paper towel and went back to his business plan.

***

"Morning, Reverend."

"Good morning, Henry."

He saved his progress, took a quick gulp of coffee and spurted it straight back out again when he saw Reverend Osbourne's latest T-shirt.

Let he who is without sin cast the first cupcake.

The reverend grinned. "Like it?"

"Love it! What can I get you this fine morning?"

"Me," Nessa said right next to Henry's ear, making him jump. "Sorry, cuz." She didn't look it.

"I thought you were out in the yard."

"I came in when I heard the bell," she said.

"Did you now." Henry eyed her suspiciously. You couldn't hear the bell from the yard.

"Yep." Nessa nodded. "Soooo…can you manage without me for a bit?"

"Why? Where are you… Oh! You, um…" Henry blushed, a bit slow on the uptake with his brain full of calculations. "Yes. Absolutely. You go. We close in an hour anyway."

"Great!" Nessa dodged around the counter, a little breathless, and smiled coyly at Reverend Osbourne.

"Thanks for this, Henry," he said.

"Anytime, Reverend." He stifled a chuckle as his ultra-confident cousin and their calm and collected vicar awkwardly negotiated their exit from the premises.

Henry Jones, Baker, est. 1874

A good, solid name, but times change, and sometimes people change with them. Even the Margaret Sharpes of this world.

Yes, the village was big enough to sustain two bakeries, but why compete when they could cooperate? The proof was in the pud…Banton Bun.

Henry refilled his coffee mug and returned once more to his business plan—*their* business plan:

Banton Bakery and Tea Rooms
Opening in 2019
(to the delight of everyone)

…guaranteeing the welcoming village of Banton, population: all kinds of folks…would always have their daily bread.

And buns.

And cakes.

For all.

The End

About Seasons of Love

Love follows no rules. Like sun in winter and rain in summer, love can blossom in the most unexpected places. This richly diverse collection of stories proves that love is as universal and as varied as the seasons.

The Stories:

- *Tourist Season* – Deven Balsam
- *Machete Betty and the Office Sharks* – Neptune Flowers
- *Once Around Seven* – Ofelia Gränd
- *Winter Blossoms* – Paul Iasevoli
- *Year of the Guilty Soul* – A.M. Leibowitz
- *The Great Village Bun Fight* – Debbie McGowan
- *A Springful of Winters* – Dawn Sister
- *Out of Season* – Bob Stone
- *Seashell Voices* – Alexis Woods
- *Courting Light* – A. Zukowski

Available as a complete anthology (ebook/paperback) and as individual stories (ebook + longer stories in paperback).

For more information/purchase links, visit:
www.beatentrackpublishing.com/SeasonsofLove

About Debbie McGowan

Debbie McGowan is an author and publisher based in a semi-rural corner of Lancashire, England. She writes character-driven, realist fiction, celebrating life, love and relationships. A working class girl, she 'ran away' to London at seventeen, was homeless, unemployed and then homeless again, interspersed with animal rights activism (all legal, honest ;)) and volunteer work as a mental health advocate. At twenty-five, she went back to college to study social science—tough with two toddlers, but they had a stay-at-home dad, so it worked itself out. These days, the toddlers are young women, and Debbie teaches undergraduate students, writes novels and runs an independent publishing company, occasionally grabbing an hour of sleep where she can.

Social Media Links

Website: debbiemcgowan.co.uk
Newsletter Signup: eepurl.com/b8emHL
Blog: deb248211.blogspot.com
Facebook: facebook.com/DebbieMcGowanAuthor and facebook.com/beatentrackpublishing
Twitter: @writerdebmcg
YouTube: youtube.com/deb248211
Instagram: instagram/writerdebmcg
Google+: plus.google.com/+DebbieMcGowan
Tumblr: writerdebmcg.tumblr.com
LinkedIn: uk.linkedin.com/in/writerdebmcg
Goodreads: goodreads.com/DebbieMcGowan

By Debbie McGowan

Checking Him Out Series

Checking Him Out (Book One)
Checking Him Out For the Holidays (Novella)
Hiding Out (Novella – Noah and Matty – HBTC Crossover)
Taking Him On (Book Two – Noah and Matty)
Checking In (Book Three)
The Making of Us (Book Four – Jesse and Leigh)

Seeds of Tyrone Series

~ co-written with Raine O'Tierney
Leaving Flowers (Book One)
Where the Grass is Greener (Book Two)
Christmas Craic and Mistletoe (Book Three)

Hiding Behind The Couch Series

The ongoing story of 'The Circle'…
Nine friends from high school;
Nine friends for life.

The Story So Far…
in chronological order:
novellas and short novels are 'stand-alone' stories, but tie in with the
series. Think Middle Earth—well, more Middle England, but with a
social conscience!

Beginnings (Novella)
Ruminations (Novel)
Class-A (Short Story)
Hiding Behind The Couch (Season One)
No Time Like The Present (Season Two)

The Harder They Fall (Season Three)
Crying in the Rain (Novel)
First Christmas (Novella)
In The Stars Part I: Capricorn–Gemini (Season Four)
Breaking Waves (Novella)
In The Stars Part II: Cancer–Sagittarius (Season Five)
A Midnight Clear (Novella)
Red Hot Christmas (Novella)
Two By Two (Season Six)
Hiding Out (Novella – CHO Crossover)
Breakfast at Cordelia's Aquarium (Short Story)
Chain of Secrets (Novella)
Those Jeffries Boys (Novel)
The WAG and The Scoundrel (Gray Fisher #1)
Reunions (Season Seven)
To Be Sure (Novella)
Tabula Rasa (Gray Fisher #2)
What A Scorcher! (Short Story)
Goth of Christmas Past (Novel)

Stand-Alone Stories

Champagne (LGBT Historical Novel)
'Time to Go' in Story Salon Big Book of Stories (Contemporary Short Story)
And The Walls Came Tumbling Down (Sci-fi Novel)
No Dice (Sci-fi Novel)
Double Six (Sci-fi Novel)
Sugar and Sawdust (M/M Romance Short Story)
Cherry Pop Valentine (M/M Romance Short Story)
Coming Up ~ co-written with Al Stewart (LGBT Short Story)
Of the Bauble (LGBT Fantasy Romance Novella)
So Long, Little Black Diamonds (Short (True) Story)
The Pastor's Last Drop (Historical Novel (Ongoing) – Wattpad)
When Skies Have Fallen (LGBT Historical Romance Novel)
A Snowy Ball (When Skies Have Fallen #1.5)
The Great Village Bun Fight (Contemporary Novella)

www.hidingbehindthecouch.com
www.debbiemcgowan.co.uk

Beaten Track Publishing

For more titles from Beaten Track Publishing,
please visit our website:

http://www.beatentrackpublishing.com

Thanks for reading!